THE LAST ENCOUNTER

Other works by Robin Maugham

Novels

THE SERVANT

LINE ON GINGER

THE ROUGH AND THE SMOOTH

BEHIND THE MIRROR

THE MAN WITH TWO SHADOWS

NOVEMBER REEF

THE GREEN SHADE

THE SECOND WINDOW

THE LINK

THE WRONG PEOPLE

Travel

COME TO DUST

NOMAD

APPROACH TO PALESTINE

NORTH AFRICAN NOTEBOOK

JOURNEY TO SIWA

THE SLAVES OF TIMBUKTU

THE JOYITA MYSTERY

Biography

SOMERSET AND ALL THE MAUGHAMS

ESCAPE FROM THE SHADOWS (AUTOBIOGRAPHY)

ROBIN MAUGHAM
THE LAST ENCOUNTER

McGraw-Hill Book Company
New York   St. Louis   San Francisco
Düsseldorf   Mexico   Toronto

Author's Note

I would like to thank Peter Burton for the
patient research he has done into General
Gordon's life and for all his help with this
book.

I have tried to be accurate. I have, however, allowed myself only one departure
from historical truth, by awarding the MM
to William Warren before this medal was
instituted.

R.M.

First published in Great Britain by W. H. Allen Ltd.,
London. First printed in the United States in 1973.
Copyright © 1972 by Robin Maugham. All rights re-
served. Printed in the United States of America. No
part of this publication may be reproduced, stored in
a retrieval system, or transmitted, in any form or by any
means, electronic, mechanical, photocopying, recording,
or otherwise, without the prior written permission of
the publisher.

123456789BPBP79876543
Library of Congress Cataloging in Publication Data

Maugham, Robin, date
  The last encounter.

  1. Gordon, Charles George, 1833-1885—Fiction.
I. Title.
PZ3.M4415Las3 [PR6025.A858]   823'.9'14   73-7534
ISBN 0-07-040967-6

For my nephew David

Observe how system into system runs,
What other planets circle other suns.
Who sees with equal eye, as God of all,
A hero perish, or a sparrow fall,
Atoms or systems into ruin hurled,
And now a bubble burst, and now a world.

ALEXANDER POPE
An Essay on Man

What is all knowledge too but recorded experience, and a product of history; of which, therefore, reasoning and belief, no less than action and passion, are essential materials.

THOMAS CARLYLE
On History

Foreword

by Colonel C. G. Luton

It is well known that while General Gordon was in Khartoum he wrote half a dozen journals which were subsequently published in England. The first of these is dated from 10 September to 23 September 1884. The last one is dated from 5 November to 14 December 1884. These journals are written in a strange mixture of schoolboy slang and biblical language. They contain not only the fifty-year-old General's comments on the military and political situation in the Sudan but also his reflections on his past experiences and his philosophy of life.

When the Dervishes invaded Khartoum on 26 January 1885 the General was killed, the Palace was burned and all documents in it were destroyed. Thus no detailed record has been available of General Gordon's actions and thoughts between 14 December 1884, and 26 January 1885.

As one of the executors of the Will of my aunt, Miss Beatrice Warren, I discovered an unbound ledger which was obviously many years old. Each page was closely covered with handwriting. The ledger was enclosed in a large manilla envelope together with a long letter from my uncle, Trooper William Warren, M.M., who had been befriended by General Gordon when he was a boy. My uncle claimed that the ledger contained the General's last journal.

My first step was to present this document for verification by the best experts I could find.

It has been conclusively proved that the pages of the ledger form the last journal that General Gordon ever wrote.

7

I have now made arrangements for the journal to be published.

Though I am not a professional editor, I realize that the General occasionally repeated some of his past utterances, but I have not changed a word that he wrote. I have, however, allowed various spellings to be amended to conform with current usage.

My reasons for publishing the work are various. The main reason—quite apart from its obvious historical interest and value—is most certainly because I believe—to quote my uncle's own words—that General Gordon's last journal deserves 'to see the light of day'.

CHARLES GEORGE LUTON
Camberley
October 1971

PART ONE

The Last Journal of General Gordon

15 December 1884

A new journal!

I am writing it in an old ledger—for there is little use for a ledger today in Khartoum.

This Journal may never see the light of day—may never be seen by any eyes except mine. I do not care. I may even destroy it—as I did my Journals in China. But I pray to God that the first six of my Khartoum Journals may reach Major Kitchener, the Adjutant of the Force that has come to relieve us in Khartoum. Kitchener is the man I have always placed my hopes upon—one of the few *very superior* British officers. He has a cool, good head and a hard constitution, combined with untiring energy.

Yesterday I despatched four of my little penny-steamers, including the *Bordein* and the *Talahawein* with my Sixth Journal. I also sent a final message to the British Relief Force stating that I expect the town to fall within three weeks. They *must* push on without delay. Our situation is desperate. Death is very close to us.

At the beginning of this Siege our situation—though precarious—was not uncomfortable. We had two million rounds of ammunition stored, and the Arsenal was capable of producing another forty thousand rounds every week. The population—including eight thousand troops—was forty-two thousand and there was food enough for all of them. Our position was strange. There was very little fighting and, though we were obviously not at peace, we didn't seem to be at war. All that has changed over these long weeks and months.

A few months ago, as I watched from the roof of the Palace, I became, each hour, more conscious of the Dervishes brooding out there, knowing they could afford to wait to starve us out. *Then* the Dervishes didn't bother much to fire on us, because we were still strong. They were content to bide their time. *Now* their fire is constant—though they have very poor aim, and their shells do little damage to the thick stone walls of the Palace. When we still had provisions, the Dervishes kept their distance. *Now*, as I watch, the huts and tents, the flags of the Dervish Emirs, inscribed with texts from the Koran and the green flag of the Mahdi, seem to creep closer across the sand. The Dervish horsemen gallop wildly between the lines. Their religious fervour continues unabated. To them, this war is a Holy War, and they are for ever prostrating themselves in prayer.

Khartoum is not a difficult town to defend. On our North, we have the Blue Nile, and on the West the White Nile— which—even at low water—is half a mile wide. Omdurman Fort is on the west bank of the White Nile. I keep my soldiers there working hard. I scan them all day through my telescope. Our weakest point is to the South where the town is open to a wide expanse of desert. Here I have dug a deep trench four miles long to link the two Niles. This area is also heavily mined and, since the Dervishes are bare-footed, I have scattered it with thousands of broken bottles.

I have had explosives placed under the Palace and in the Arsenal so that, in the event of an attack, both could be blown up. I may soon be forced to make that decision.

I daily pray that the Relief Expedition will arrive. I must fulfil my promises to the people of Khartoum. The treatment they would receive at the Mahdi's hands would be horrible in its cruelty.

17 December

Not much news from our outposts. A little sniping—that's all. A mule has escaped from the Mahdi's forces and has come in to our lines. Unfortunately it gave no information about the Dervishes' strength. But from its action we can definitely assume that it no longer believes in the Mahdi.

This evening I suddenly felt hungry. I wanted some supper, for I hadn't eaten all day. I rang the bell. No answer. I rang it again. Still no answer. If one's Sudanese servants are not eating, they are saying their prayers. If they're not saying their prayers, they're sleeping. If they're not sleeping, they are sick. One snatches at them at intervals. You want to send an immediate order, and there is your servant bobbing up and down in prayer, and you can't disturb him. The Sudan is really a beautiful country for trying experiments with your patience.

Why do I write such strange nonsense in these journals of mine? One reason is most surely that I find it painful to face the truth—which is this: if the Expeditionary Force does not come within three weeks, Khartoum will fall. We are surrounded by the Mahdi's forces which increase daily. We are short of food. For instance, we have less than eighty thousand okes of biscuit for the whole population, and an oke is three pounds in weight. My only communication with the outside world lies in the three river steamers. But the Dervishes line the banks of the Nile, and each time one of my poor little penny-steamers leaves I am on tenterhooks for it. Only last week the *Bordein* was struck by a shell, but only one man was wounded.

I sit, hour by hour, at this desk in my narrow bedroom, staring out over the river. I sit here because, after I have inspected the outposts, there is so very little else that I can do—except wait. Next door is what I call my Operational Headquarters which I converted from one of the main rooms of the Governor's Palace. We once used part of it as a mess-room when the others were still here—ten months ago. But now they have gone—every single one of them.

I wander out on to the verandah and look through the little telescope—or I climb up to the roof and gaze through the larger telescope I have fixed there. From the roof I can survey the Blue Nile and its confluence with the White Nile, and I can see my fort at Omdurman quite clearly. Below me lie the dun-coloured mud-houses of the town and the dry, dusty alleys between them. The heat oppresses me. After a while, I feel so low and dispirited that I climb downstairs and help myself to a brandy and soda.

The Mahdi's revolt was inevitable. It sprung out of a general resurgence of a movement spreading throughout the Islamic countries, which was bred out of the European repression of the national interests of the Islamic peoples. It was inevitable that it would happen. Sooner or later, anyone should have been able to foretell, one of the Islamic nations would rise up and try to throw off the yokes of their oppressors. Because of the fanatically intense Mohammedanism of the Sudanese, we should have realised that the first serious revolt would be in the Sudan. But I confess this. When I was in England, I hadn't appreciated how powerful the Mahdi is—or the hold he has over his people.

I still feel—maybe optimistically—that the Mahdist forces can be smashed up *if* the Expeditionary Force would make haste. The sight of only one redcoat would be enough to frighten the Dervishes away from Khartoum. Then, as they retreated, we could push them further and further back and, in the end, we could destroy them completely.

Maybe this is not to be so. It is possible that this is not God's Will.

Why did I ever come out to Khartoum? Why did I ever accept the post of Governor-General of the Sudan? What does the Sudan have to offer any European?

The Sudan is the largest country in Africa—almost as large as the entire of Europe combined. Yet it is a neglected country, a political and economic backwater, defended against the outside world by its swamps and deserts. The South of the Sudan, the Equatorial Province, is sticky, wet and green. The North is dry and arid, and the people have to depend on the rise and fall of the Nile to enable them to raise crops. In the South they have heavy, tropical rainfall; in the North it hardly ever rains. There are, in fact, two Sudans. The African Sudan—in the South; and the Arab Sudan—in the North.

Whatever governmental structure any European or civilised country may attempt to impose on the Sudan stands little hope of success. For the country still clings to the tribal unit of rule. There are the tribes that raise crops along the banks of the Nile; there are tribes that live in the towns along the river's banks—Dongola, Berber, Kosti and here in Khartoum. There are cattle-owning tribes, and there are nomadic camel-owning tribes who wander the eternal wastes of this country looking for water and pasturelands for their beasts.

The country is crippled by disease and poverty. The Sudanese suffer from sleeping sickness, guinea-worm, yellow fever, leprosy, malaria and bilharziasis. Life expectancy is little more than thirty years. The people are not only oppressed by disease and poverty, they have been harried and ill-treated by their Egyptian overlords, who have treated this country as a cloth that is soaked and must be wrung dry until every drop of precious water is gone.

It is a hideous, harsh and cruel country. Nothing grows green. Everything is yellow—bleached by the merciless sun. Besides elephants, lions, giraffe, crocodiles, hippopotamuses, there are numerous loathsome bugs that fly or crawl—devouring white ants, tarantulas, scorpions and snakes. It is a quarter of a vast continent composed of ignorance and sheer squalor.

The Sudan is an accursed wilderness, an empty limbo of torment for ever and ever. The Dervishes have a saying that God laughed when he had created the Sudan. It is easy to understand why.

All the Sudanese have to sustain them in their harsh existence is their fierce belief in God. They are intensely, fanatically religious.

What was it that brought me back to this country which I thought I would never see again? Why did I accept this position of Governor-General? I could so easily have stayed in obscurity on the shelf happily pottering around with my Biblical explorations and studies. Or I could have gone to the Congo . . .

Was it the persuasion of my sister Augusta? Or was it the impetuous enthusiasm of Stead and his newspaper? Or was it some intense feeling of my own destiny which drove me out here to this filthy, barren place?

18 December

My belief is that the Mahdi's war will be the end of slavery in the Sudan. The Arabs have invariably put their slaves in the front and armed them; and the slaves have seen that they were plucky, while their masters shirked. It is unlikely that these slaves will ever yield to those masters as heretofore.

The night is unusually quiet. In my fancy I can almost hear

the stirrings and firm breathing of the twenty thousand Dervishes who surround us.

Once again my mind is plagued to discover the reason why I ever came out here, and my thoughts—perhaps quickened by brandy—lurch back to that fatal day of my return to England from Palestine. It seems an age ago. Yet in fact it was on the seventh of January of this very year of our Lord, 1884.

Nothing seemed to have changed about our house in Rockstone Place, Southampton, when I arrived back from Palestine.

Mary, our maid, when she answered the front-door, was as plump and rosy-cheeked as ever. Augusta—my dear sister —was waiting for me in the drawing-room, looking as dignified and as austere as ever, bless her heart. I now see little of my family—apart from Augusta to whom I am devoted. I was one of the youngest in a family of eleven children. I was the fourth son. My father was descended from Scottish Highlanders. He was an officer in the Royal Artillery. While he was on active service we never had a settled home. We moved from Woolwich, where I was born, to Dublin, then to Leith. From Leith we moved to Corfu, and finally back to Woolwich. My mother was strictly religious, and Augusta—my elder sister—takes after her. As the family had been in the Army for three generations it was obvious that I would make it my career. But in those days, when I was at Woolwich Academy, which I entered when I was fifteen, I was hot-tempered, and undisciplined. My ill-temper lost me a vacancy in the Royal Artillery. I had to be content with a position in the Royal Engineers.

I have been a nomad most of my life. I therefore appreciate all the more the familiar security of Augusta's home. The room, with its unusually hard sofas and armchairs, and its sturdy furniture, seemed also to be unaltered. But I noticed that there had been one change. On the wall above the roll-topped desk, Augusta had hung a large map of the Sudan.

I knew that Augusta was delighted to see me. I also divined—quite correctly as it turned out—that she would be quite determined not to show a glimmer of her excitement.

'You're thinner,' Augusta said. 'Do you want to wash?'

'Do I look particularly dirty?' I asked her.

'No,' she replied. 'But you've had a long journey.'

'Fortunately,' I said, 'there was plenty of water on the ship.'

Then I crossed the room and kissed her. Out of the corner of my eye I noticed a telegram lying on the table. I could guess from whom it came. I could also guess that Augusta was longing to tell me about it. But as yet I didn't feel inclined even to consider the matter.

'Did you get my last letter from Jaffa?' I asked her. 'About Noah's Ark? I've found the site of it. The Ark definitely came to rest on Mount Moriah.'

'Charlie,' Augusta broke in, 'a telegram arrived for you this morning, and I opened it.'

'Mount Ararat of Armenia never was the true site,' I continued firmly. 'There's not a word in the Scriptures to suggest that Armenia had anything to do with Israel.'

'Charlie,' Augusta said, with a trace of severity in her expression which reminded me of my childhood, 'the telegram was from W. T. Stead, Editor of the *Pall Mall Gazette* —now one of the most influential newspapers in the country. He wants your opinion on the Sudan crisis.'

'So he told me in the telegraph he sent to my ship,' I answered. 'But I telegraphed him back to say that my opinions aren't sufficiently important to warrant his journey-ing down here.'

Patiently I explained to Augusta that it was well over four years since I had been in the Sudan in an attempt to stamp out the slave trade. I pointed out to her that I was no longer in touch with events, and that the diplomatists and powers-that-be detested me. I was no longer 'Chinese Gordon', leading the so-called Ever-Victorious Army to victory over the Taipings. I was a back number. What had I, in fact, achieved in these last five years? Set off for Abyssinia and failed in my mission. Left for India as a private secretary to the Viceroy and chucked up the job after only three days. Gone back to China and given it up after five weeks. Acted as Commanding Engineer in Mauritius for ten months. Not bad, but hardly distinguished. Five months in South Africa trying to help the Basutos. Hopeless. And then a year pottering around Palestine. Not an impressive record.

'But I don't care,' I told Augusta. 'I've got other plans. Why do you think King Leopold asked me to stop in Brussels on my way home? Because he wants me to join Stanley in the Congo—to end slavery there once and for all. I shall go out as Second-in-Command. That will be the last work I shall do.'

Augusta gazed at me for a while in silence. There was a slight tremor in her voice when she spoke again.

'Are you certain that this is God's Will?' she asked.

'Why should you doubt it?' I replied. 'To begin with, the British Government would never consent to employ me. The new Khedive of Egypt doesn't like me. And that's an end to it. You've hung up the wrong map, Augusta.'

'That remains to be seen.'

'Don't egg ambition on in me,' I said. 'Try to drown it.'

But Augusta wasn't listening. She was staring through the lace curtains out of the window.

'What time did you send off your telegraph?' she suddenly asked. 'A carriage has drawn up in front of our door and a grey-haired man has got out. If it *is* Mr Stead, will you see him?'

'If he's come all the way down from London,' I answered, 'I can hardly refuse. But I shall warn him he's wasting his time.'

A few moments later Mary came in and announced Mr W. T. Stead. The man introduced himself to us and apologised for his intrusion.

I had heard that he was born of God-fearing, Non-Conformist stock and had devoted himself to the career of journalism with the zeal of a Crusader. Stead was short, sparely-built and bearded, with an eager face and keen, piercing eyes. He was very plainly dressed. In fact, at first sight, there was nothing unusual about him. After a few seconds, however, I became aware that beneath his impetuous manner some part of him seemed to glow with a fanatical enthusiasm and an intense religious conviction.

'I have come here,' he said to me, 'because I want your views on the crisis in the Sudan.'

I told him, as I had told Augusta earlier, that I was no longer an expert since I had left the place more than four years ago.

'Mr Gladstone was never in the Sudan in his life,' Stead replied. 'But that does not prevent him from giving the world his opinions on the matter.'

'You have no high opinion of our Prime Minister?' I asked.

'He is a man of virtue and a crafty hypocrite.' Stead answered. 'He is as hard as a rock and as soft as a serpent. He is admired and despised. He is a great man, and I do not trust him. But I am here to find out about the Sudan—not to sum up Mr Gladstone's oddly mixed character. I have come to listen, not to preach.' He paused. 'Have you seen the despatch from Cairo that was printed this morning?' he demanded.

I told him that I hadn't. I asked him what it contained.

Stead spoke slowly and deliberately. ' "It is believed in Cairo," ' he quoted, ' "that our Government has decided to abandon Khartoum and the whole of the Sudan." '

I stared at him in amazement. 'There must be a mistake,' I said.

'The despatch was printed in *The Times* this morning.'

'Their correspondent must have gone mad!'

'You have been abroad a year, General Gordon,' Stead remarked. 'The Government's policy has changed radically in that time.'

'After the effort and sacrifice we have made to deliver the people from slavery,' I said, 'do you believe that the Government intends to abandon the Sudan?'

'Yes,' Stead replied quietly. 'As a result of the Mahdi's successful revolt it's now considered wiser to persuade the Egyptian Government to withdraw to their own frontiers, fortify them and stand there.'

'Do *you* believe that?' I asked him.

'In my editorial comment,' he answered, 'I can only say that I believe it is far better to withdraw and stand fast than to remain in the Sudan and crumble.'

I started to speak quietly, but gradually I couldn't help becoming more heated, more excited. I began to pace up and down the room.

'You have six thousand men in Khartoum,' I said. 'What are you going to do with them? Are they to be sacrificed? Their only offence is their loyalty to their Sovereign. For their fidelity are you going to abandon them to their fate?'

'Couldn't they be withdrawn to Wadi Halfa?' Stead suggested.

'How on earth can you move six thousand men from Khartoum—through the desert to Wadi Halfa?' I asked. 'Where are you going to get the camels to take them away? Will the Mahdi supply them? The garrison won't be allowed to leave with a coat on their backs. The Dervishes will plunder them to the skin. Even their lives won't be spared. Whatever you may decide about the possibility of evacuation, you can't evacuate, because the army can't be moved. As for fortifying the Egyptian frontier, it's no more than a line in the desert. You might as well fortify against a fever. No. You must either surrender absolutely to the Mahdi or defend Khartoum at all hazards.'

'Which would you do?' Stead asked.

'Surrender is unthinkable,' I said. 'Hold on to the Eastern Sudan with Khartoum as headquarters, and you will keep the Nile. And then the Mahdi's forces will fall to pieces of themselves.'

'But the natives believe he's the prophet—the Messiah they have awaited for so long,' Stead pointed out. 'They follow him with the devotion of fanatics.'

'There have been false prophets long before Mohamet Ahmed, the boat-builder's nephew, claimed he was the Mahdi—the long-awaited prophet,' I said. 'They come and go. It was I who laid the egg this so-called Messiah has hatched, because I taught the people they had rights. Everything has sprung from that. Why has this fanatic Mahdi gained so many supporters? Why is the Sudan in revolt? For the same reason that any other country revolts. Because of oppressive rule. The Khedive's forces have plundered and oppressed the people of the Sudan. Oppression breeds discontent. Discontent means an increase of the armed forces. That means an increase of expenditure which has to be met by more taxation. And that still further increases the discontent. And so things have gone on and on in a dismal circle until they have culminated in this disastrous rebellion. The rebellion was caused by injustice and wrong treatment. The way to overcome rebellion is to remove the wrong and do the right thing for the people. Reduce their taxation. Rescue them from the money-lenders. Remove the instruments of their oppression.'

'How can that be done?' Stead asked.

'Appoint a Governor-General at Khartoum,' I told him. 'Furnish him with two million sterling. It's a large sum. But a sum which had much better be spent now than wasted in a vain attempt to avert the catastrophe of an ill-timed surrender.'

Stead spoke very quietly. 'When would you be ready to go?' he asked me.

'I'm not the man to choose,' I told him. 'Besides, I'm not free. I'm joining Stanley in the Congo.'

Augusta looked up at Mr Stead. 'We are uncertain,' she murmured. 'We don't know what my brother should do. We would be grateful for your help.'

Stead raised his head as if he were listening to another, more distant voice.

'General Gordon, I told you I thought I could help you,' he said slowly. 'I should have told you that I *know* I can. Before I left London this morning I saw the Foreign Secretary. I am empowered to inform you that a strong section of the Cabinet is in favour of your employment in the Sudan. But before these men press their views they must be certain that you would accept to go back as Governor-General.'

'I can't be party to an intrigue,' I told him.

'Nor, sir, can I,' he answered. 'But this is no intrigue. These Ministers are convinced that you are the only man for the task. They only await your consent before they put their views openly and honestly before the Cabinet.'

'These men—what are their names?' I enquired.

'Granville, Hartington, Northbrook, Dilke and lastly Wolseley—their military adviser and your friend,' he answered.

'Can they sway the Cabinet? Can they persuade Gladstone to change his policy?' I asked.

'No,' he answered.

'Then what good can they do by their attempt?'

'Alone they cannot succeed,' was his reply. 'But they will not be alone—because within a week I shall have seen to it that every voter in this country has the chance to decide for himself whether you, General Gordon, should be sent to the Sudan or not. I know what their decision will be.'

'How can you be sure?' Augusta asked him.

'Because tomorrow in the *Pall Mall Gazette* I shall start a campaign that will be remembered for all time in the annals of the Press,' Stead announced. 'I was uncertain before I came here. But now I know. I see what I must do.'

Stead turned his gaze towards me. His eyes were shining.

'You are the man I hoped to find,' he said. 'You are the only person now who can save the Sudan. Within a week, in every club and public house they will know it. The other papers will be quick to join in the campaign. Soon all of England, from Land's End to John O'Groats, will be repeating five words, the five words of my headline: "Chinese Gordon for the Sudan".'

'How can you be certain that I am the right man?' I asked.

'Some instinct sent me to you,' Stead answered. 'I know, now, whence it came. All this was meant to be. I feel it in my soul.'

He paused and then deliberately took a pace towards me.

'General Gordon,' he said, 'if the Government asks you, will you consent to go to the Sudan—however dangerous the mission may be?'

For an instant there was complete silence. Stead's eyes were fixed on me, and I knew that Augusta was watching me intently, her hands clasped tightly together. When I replied, it was as if it were some other voice than my own which answered.

'Yes,' I heard myself say.

I have now rehearsed the whole scene that led to my acceptance, and I'm still uncertain about what finally made me agree to go.

It is possible that just in the same way that memory makes us forget the pains we have suffered in our life, so there may be some force in our souls which prevents us from understanding our true motives because it would be too painful to admit them?

The Dervishes fired two shells at the Palace this morning. One shell burst in the air; the other fell in the river in direct line with the window I was sitting at.

Three of my Arab soldiers deserted to the Dervishes today. But I discovered that these men had previously served with the Mahdi's forces and had now only returned to them.

There is little of military importance to write in this journal, for the situation each day remains largely unchanged. We are surrounded; we shall soon run out of food and ammunition.

At various hours of the day I inspect our defences. Then I return to my room in the Palace. I walk out on to the balcony and look through my telescope, hoping with all my heart to see the smoke of a steamer coming up the river.

The bleakness of the prospect before me makes my mind seek relief by turning back to the security of the last few days I spent in England, in Rockstone Place, with Augusta.

One incident has remained very sharply impressed in my memory . . .

The morning after Stead's visit, when we were awaiting a decision from the Cabinet, I was sitting in the drawing-room drinking coffee with Augusta—and wishing it were brandy— when Mary, the young maid, interrupted us.

'Mr Hopkin is downstairs to see you, Miss Augusta,' she announced.

Augusta put down her cup of coffee. 'Mr Hopkin, is a teacher at the Mission School,' she explained. 'I'll go down to see him. I won't be long.'

For once I had a feeling there was something a little secretive in Augusta's manner. Why didn't she want me to meet Hopkin? Was she ashamed of him? Or had a faint perfume of romance wafted into her life at the age of sixty-three?

'Ask Mr Hopkin to come up,' I said to Mary.

I noticed that Augusta's mouth tightened as Mary left the room.

'You won't like him.' she said.

'How do you know?' I asked.

'In fact I'm not at all sure he's the right man for the job,' Augusta continued. 'He's far too sensitive. You know what I mean. These boys at the school are the dregs of the town— run-aways from lighters and barley boats, riff-raff from the poorest quarters. Their wretched lives have made them tough and heartless.'

'Have you had trouble?' I enquired.

Augusta nodded. 'And poor Hopkin isn't the man to deal with it,' she said. 'Don't frighten him, will you?'

I laughed. 'Am I so frightening?' I asked.

'To those who don't know you—yes.' Augusta answered flatly.

As she spoke Hopkin rushed in. I saw a plump, middle-aged man with large spaniel eyes, a long nose and a weak mouth. A grubby handkerchief, slightly stained with blood, was bound around his forehead. He looked pale and distraught.

'Miss Augusta,' he said. 'Heaven be praised I found you . . .'

Then he turned and saw me. He gave a little shiver of surprise.

'Forgive me,' he said. 'I had no idea. I thought . . . that is to say . . . I supposed you were alone.'

He moved nervously towards me and shook my hand. 'Please forgive this intrusion, General Gordon,' he said. 'I can return later.'

'You're most welcome, Mr Hopkin,' I said. Then I glanced at his forehead. 'I fear you've had an accident.'

'Please forgive these domestic matters, General,' he stammered. 'But I've reached the limit of my endurances. I can go on no longer. As you can see I've been severely wounded. He's a real brute. Vicious and Godless.'

'Who is this person?' I asked. 'Explain yourself.'

'Scott is his name,' Hopkin said. 'He hates me and all that I stand for. Each time he appears I know he'll break up my class. If he sees the chance, I know he'll come back again tomorrow. I know he will. He's a bad lot.'

'Then he deserves to be put into gaol,' I said.

'That's precisely what I want,' Hopkin replied promptly. 'We've got him in custody downstairs at this moment. I came to ask Miss Augusta's permission to hand him over to the police.'

I turned to Augusta. 'I would have thought there was no question about it,' I announced.

'Thank you, sir,' said Hopkin. He turned to go.

'One moment, Mr Hopkin,' Augusta said quietly. 'Are you referring to Harry Scott?'

'Certainly,' replied Hopkin.

'Well then, would you mind telling my brother what Harry Scott's age is?' Augusta asked.

'What has a man's age got to do with it?' I enquired.

Hopkin looked embarrassed. 'I'd hardly call him a man,' he said. 'He's . . . well, in fact he's sixteen.'

I laughed. 'I'd imagined a bearded villain at least six foot tall.'

For once Augusta smiled. 'I thought you did,' she said.

I looked again at the bandage round Mr Hopkin's head. 'But how did he inflict that wound?' I asked.

Grimly Hopkin produced from his pocket a large home-made catapult.

'With this,' he replied.

I examined the weapon. It was intricately made. 'Very ingenious,' I remarked.

'Oh, he's ingenious enough,' Hopkin said. 'He has the cunning of the devil.'

'And this monster is in custody downstairs?' I asked.

'Yes,' Hopkin nodded.

'What were you teaching in your class today?' I enquired.

'A lesson from the Holy Scriptures,' he answered. 'Elijah and the ravens.'

I asked if I could see the boy, but Hopkin protested that it would be a waste of my time. Then he paused.

'Unless, of course, he knew that he was in the presence of General Gordon . . .' he began.

I interrupted him. 'He will listen to me for what I believe, not for what I'm supposed to have done,' I said. 'You will not tell him my name. Anyhow, I doubt if he's heard of it. Will you please send him up to me?'

'Charlie, let's leave it until tomorrow,' Augusta said.

'No. I'd like to see the boy now,' I replied. 'And I do suggest, Augusta, that you should put a clean bandage round Mr Hopkin's forehead.'

Augusta hesitated. But Hopkin had already opened the door for her. She gave me a smile which was half affectionate and half vexed. Then she and Hopkin left the room.

A few minutes later, the door opened and an impudent-looking boy slouched in. He stood, with his hands deep in his pockets, watching me with hostility. His shirt was dirty and torn. His face was bruised. He was evidently tough. But I felt I could see an odd look of yearning in his wide-set eyes. I was immediately attracted to him.

Obviously I can't remember every word of our conversation, but I shall set it down as best as I can.

'So you're Harry Scott?' I said.

'That's it,' he answered.

'What's your job?' I asked.

'Got none just now,' the boy replied.

'Why do you go to the Mission School?' I asked.

'Nothing better to do, I suppose,' was his answer. 'The rooms are warm and they give us soup.'

'Why don't you like Mr Hopkin?' I enquired.

''Cos he acts soft and talks soft like the rest of them,' the boy replied. Then he moved towards me. 'Look, Mister, get it over and done with,' he said. 'Give me the beating and let me go.'

'I'm not going to beat you,' I said.

'So it's the coppers again now, is it?' he said in his strange husky voice. 'Can't you make up your mind?'

'We're not going to the police,' I told him.

'Then what do you want?' he asked.

'To show you kindness,' I replied.

' "To show you kindness," ' he mimicked. 'You're just another of them. I might have known.'

The boy was gazing at me in contempt. Suddenly I tried to see myself as he would be seeing me. I realised that the suit I was wearing was shabby and the cuffs were frayed. Though I am of slender build I am now fifty years old. To the boy I must have appeared a seedy old man—even though there was only a touch of grey in my hair and in my whiskers. Perhaps he thought that there was a weakness in the expression of my rather large blue eyes.

At that moment, I made up my mind that I would try to win the boy over to my side—without the use of either force or authority.

'Are your father and mother alive?' I asked him.

'Suppose so,' the boy replied.

'But you don't live at home?'

He gave a short laugh. 'And get a belting every night,' he said. 'Not likely.'

'Has Mr Hopkin done anything to harm you?' I enquired.

'I'd like to see him try,' Harry said.

'Then why did you break up his class?' I asked.

''Cos he was talking rot,' Harry said. 'Whoever heard of a man being fed by birds? Flap, flap. Caw, caw. And here's yer dinner, Elijer. Load of old tommy-rot.'

I smiled at his mocking face.

'I'd have told you a different story from the Holy Scriptures,' I announced. Indeed, it was one of my favourite stories to tell on the rare occasions when I had time to teach the boys at Augusta's missionary school.

'So you're a preacher too?' the boy asked.

'In a way,' I said.

'What's your name, Mister?'

'Gordon,' I said.

'Any relation to "Chinese Gordon"?' the boy asked with a slight show of interest.

'Yes,' I answered.

The boy's voice was sneering. 'I'll bet it's distant,' he said.

I smiled at him, and as I smiled I stared into the boy's eyes. They were hazel-coloured and wonderfully bright.

'My story's about a boy of your age,' I began. 'This lad was with the Army out in Palestine some years ago. And the enemy sent out their champion fighter to challenge any man from his side. Their champion was a great giant of a man called Goliath. He was so huge and so fierce that not one of them dared to take him on.'

I was still gazing at Harry's face. I could see that, as yet, he was not interested, but he seemed a bit surprised at the calmness and certainty of my voice.

'The enemy were jeering at them,' I continued. 'Then this boy of your age went to the King, and he said: "Let me go. I'm small, but God will help me." So the boy advanced across the plain to meet this giant. Now Goliath had got a great sword and a long spear. But this boy of sixteen—David his name was—had got no armour. All he had was his faith in God. And he also had . . .'

I paused. Then slowly I produced the catapult from my pocket and turned it over admiringly. Harry stared at me in amazement.

'No joking?' he said.

'He had this simple and ingenious weapon,' I told him.

'He went for the giant with a catapult?' Harry asked. 'And what then?'

I could remember the text by heart.

'Goliath drew nigh to meet David,' I said, 'and David put his hand in his bag and took thence a stone, and slung it. And the stone sunk into the giant's forehead; and he fell upon his face to the earth. And David ran and took his sword and drew it out of the sheath and killed him. And when the enemy saw their champion was dead, they fled.'

Harry was now staring at me.

'Mr Hopkin can tell you the rest,' I said. 'But the point of the story is this. You may be tough. You may be stronger than anyone else around you. But if there's wrong in your heart you will fall like Goliath. You may be small like David. You may be all alone and people may jeer at you. But if in your heart you know you're right, then God will give you strength.'

I suppose I could say that this has been my creed throughout my life. At any rate, I found my voice was firm with conviction. Harry was now watching me with fascination. I looked at him and smiled.

'When did you last have something to eat?' I asked him.

'Soup this morning,' the boy said.

I took out a florin from my pocket and gave it to Harry.

'Go down to Mr Hopkin and tell him you're sorry,' I said. 'Then go and get yourself something to eat. Now be off with you.'

I turned away from him. But Harry did not move.

'Mister,' he said. 'Mister Gordon. Can I take this with me?'

I turned. The boy was pointing to the catapult which I had left on the table.

'Do you promise me you won't use it on birds—or Missionaries?' I asked.

For the first time Harry smiled. 'Yes, Mister,' he promised me. It may have been his smile which influenced my final decision.

'Very well,' I said. 'Take it.'

I turned to the map of the Sudan. But Harry still did not move.

'Thanks for the cash,' he said in his surprisingly deep and husky voice.

Slowly I turned round to look at him. His face was tough, but his eyes were strangely gentle.

'Where do you live?' I asked.

'No place,' he mumbled.

'Where do you sleep?'

'In boats mostly,' he said. 'Sometimes in the park.'

I crossed the room and pulled the bell.

'Where are your parents?' I asked the boy.

'In Liverpool,' he answered. 'I ran away. Dad beat me.'

'Can you saw up firewood?' I enquired.

He nodded.

'Good,' I said. 'That's what you'll be doing till we get you fit enough to join the Colours.'

'Who says I'm going to enlist?' Harry asked.

'I do,' I said. 'But we'll talk about that later.'

As I spoke, Mary came in.

'Take this young ruffian down to the cook,' I told Mary. 'Tell her to give him a good scrubbing. She can find him clean clothes out of my store. He can sleep in the attic.'

Mary showed no trace of surprise. I'd given help and shelter to boys before. I walked up to Harry and put my arm on his shoulder.

'I want to see a new person—without and within,' I told him. 'Now cut along.'

I went back to the map. Harry did not move. I turned back to him. He was staring at me in bewilderment.

'Come on,' Mary said to him. 'You heard what the General said.'

I could almost see the word sinking into the boy's consciousness.

'General?' he repeated. Then he looked up at me with a kind of awe. 'General,' he said. 'General Gordon.'

Mary gave a slight shrug of her shoulders. Obviously she thought the boy must be weak in the head. She led him, unprotesting, out of the room.

21 December

I have found at least some measure of release from the present by recalling the events from less than a year ago.

I now feel an urge to bring the story of these last months up to the present day.

On 18 January I had a meeting at the War Office in London. Most of the Cabinet, including Gladstone, who was ill, were out of town. However, two Ministers were present: Lord Granville, the Foreign Secretary, and Lord Hartington, the Secretary of State for War. Also present were Earl Northbrook, the First Lord of the Admiralty, and Sir Charles Dilke, President of the Local Government Board, who had, during the earlier period of Gladstone's ministry worked as Under-Secretary for Foreign Affairs.

By then I had had time for discussions with various friends in London, so I was not surprised by what took place at the meeting. I had a preliminary talk with Sir Garnet Wolseley in the ante-room in which he explained the Cabinet's position. Then he led me into the room in which they were meeting. I was asked if I had understood Wolseley's ideas. I said I did. I repeated what he had said, which was that the Government should evacuate the Sudan. They seemed pleased and said that this was their idea. They asked me if I would go. I said, 'Yes'. They said, 'When?' I answered, 'Tonight'. And it was over.

At the end of the meeting I presented each of them with a book I hoped they would find edifying. It was *Scripture Promises* by Dr Samuel Clarke.

That very evening I left London from Charing Cross Station. Lord Granville himself bought my ticket. Wolseley himself carried my hand-baggage. The Commander-in-Chief, His Royal Highness the Duke of Cambridge, held open the carriage door for me. Such had been my hurry that I discovered I had forgotten to bring any money with me. Whereupon—to my surprise—Wolseley emptied his own pockets and handed over all his spare cash together with his gold pocket-watch and chain.

Travelling with me to Calais, en route to the Sudan, was Colonel J. D. H. Stewart, who, being the most experienced help-mate available, had been assigned to me as Military Secretary and Second-in-Command. Stewart was a tall man, with slightly myopic eyes, and a neatly clipped moustache. He was possessed of a typical Cavalry Officer's energy. This was combined with a cool head, patience—unusual in a Scot —and a fair comprehension of Moslem politics. Only the year previously he had been in the Sudan for some months— on a slightly mysterious Military Mission. Beneath the obviously conventional façade I suspected Stewart to be very ambitious.

As the train left London a package containing a sealed order had been given to me. When I opened it I found that my instructions were to perform in the Sudan such other duties as the Egyptian Government might desire to entrust to me or such as might be communicated to me by Sir Evelyn Baring, the British Commissioner in Cairo.

This of course opened up a whole world of possibilities.

I spent a hectic forty-eight hours in Cairo. I had several meetings with Baring. I had met him before. On the occasions of our previous meetings, our relations had been far from cordial. I had, in fact, disliked him on sight. I rather suspect his feelings about me were of a similar nature. He seemed to have a patronising attitude towards me, hidden beneath the professional veneer of reserve and the cool, careful and calm attitude of the perfect diplomatist. Baring hadn't liked it when I'd gone rather over his head in my attempts to help sort out the muddle of the Khedive's affairs. *That*—he had assured me—was *his* province. I had been rebuffed and sent back to Khartoum. That was all in the past, however, and, whilst I was in Cairo for those forty-eight hours, Baring made every effort to be civil and helpful. It was only later that he proved himself unreliable and unhelpful. Oil and water don't mix. Nor will I ever mix with Baring.

One curious incident occurred while I was in Cairo. Almost as soon as I arrived I ran into Zubair, quite by chance. Zubair had been the most famous slaver in the Sudan when I'd been here five years ago, to suppress the trade at a time when seven-eighths of the population were slaves. In those days, Zubair was so powerful that he was virtually king of a widespread district.

I had a strange sense that he might have reformed since those days. I couldn't get the man out of my mind. Suddenly an idea came to me. Why should I not take Zubair with me to Khartoum to rally opposition to the Mahdi?

That very evening, I mentioned my plan to Baring. He admitted that it had its advantages but was dismayed by the thought of the reaction in England if I used a slaver to reconquer the Sudan.

On the morning of 18 February the little paddle-steamer on which I was travelling—the *Tewifieh*—was first seen by the people of Khartoum at the junction of the Blue and the White Niles. At 9.30 a.m. I arrived at the landing-stage outside the Palace.

It was with very mixed emotions that I landed at Khartoum —once again Governor-General. I had left Khartoum five years before, in 1879, thinking never to return. Here I stood again, on the same landing-stage—and the people remembered me, remembered me as a just and patient ruler.

My entry into Khartoum was marked by a scene of indescribable enthusiasm and public confidence. Thousands of the inhabitants—it seemed to be the whole population—crowded down to the riverside to greet me. Men, women and children, with their splendidly brown skins and white jellabahs, thronged about me as I walked to the Palace. The crowds pressed about me calling me 'Father' and 'Sultan'. They kissed my hands, and the women threw themselves on the ground at my feet. In the confusion I was several times pushed down. This remarkable demonstration continued for the entire length of the walk.

They all seemed to welcome me as a conqueror and deliverer, though I had really come in my own person to deal with a desperate situation.

We have nothing further to do, when the scroll of events is unrolled, than to accept them as being for the best . . . But what man really knows himself—who can tell his true motives? Or the motives of others? I can't even understand the motives of the inhabitants of Khartoum . . . I find it is wonderful how the people of the town, who have every facility to leave, cling to it. What can their motives now be? There are hundreds who flock in, though it is an open secret we have little money or food.

The first thing I did on that February morning so many months ago was to inspect the town's defences. I could see at once the improvements which should be made. Then, I prepared my bonfire. I ordered to be piled into a heap in front of the Palace all the Government books, recording from time immemorial the outstanding debts of the over-taxed people. I made the native officers collect all the kourbashes, whips and lashes, each wooden instrument for bastinado, and to add them to the pile. Then I returned to the Palace.

The main room, on the first floor of the Governor-General's Palace in Khartoum, is furnished in the ornate style of the period. One or two pieces of simple English furniture have obviously been imported by previous occupants. This room I decided to convert partly into an Operational Headquarters and partly into a Mess-room. Wide French windows lead out on to the broad verandah, which stretches the whole length of the Palace. Beyond one can see the tops of the palm trees in the garden below. The room next door I decided to use as my study and my bedroom. A desk had already been placed in it, and I sat down to write my first report. It's strange to think that that afternoon was *over ten months ago*. I have just looked up the date again. It was on 18 February.

While I was writing I couldn't help overhearing some of my officers talking in the adjoining room. But did that help me to understand their motives? Very little, I fear . . . Too little, in fact.

I could hear that De Coetlogon, the British General, was having a chinwag with Herbin, the French Consul. De Coetlogon, then the Commanding Officer of Khartoum, was a large, red-faced, middle-aged English gentleman (despite his name) with a bluff, yet haughty manner. At our first meeting that morning, I had sensed that he was very conscious of his own importance. Herbin was a slim, urbane Frenchman of about forty, meticulously dressed, with a neat, pointed beard. Though his manner was cynical and sometimes malicious I suspected he was generally kind, and well-disposed towards me. He spoke very precise English with only a slight accent.

'I hope he's not going to keep us waiting much longer,' De Coetlogon was saying. 'I want to get back to my wife.

I should never have let her come out here. But thank heavens we'll be leaving soon.'

'You think so?' Herbin asked.

'What makes you doubt it?' De Coetlogon replied.

'The people this morning,' Herbin answered. 'You weren't on the *quai* when he arrived.'

'I heard the usual song and dance going on,' De Coetlogon answered.

'Song and dance, yes,' Herbin replied. 'Usual, no.'

'Pure hysteria,' De Coetlogon exclaimed. 'It won't last. "Father and Saviour of the Sudan" indeed! They'll hate him within a fortnight. He wasn't popular when he was here last time—I can tell you that. They think he can crush the Mahdi. But they're wrong. No man can.'

I could almost see his red jowls quivering as he spoke.

'Listen to me, Herbin,' he went on. 'You're French Consul here. Your job is concerned with civilians. I'm Commander of the Garrison. My job is with the troops. I know the men under me. And I can tell you that at least a third of them are unreliable. The sooner we get out of Khartoum, the better.'

A few moments later, when I entered the room, my Second-in-Command, Colonel Stewart, had joined the two of them and was standing looming over them both with his usual dour expression.

'Where is Mr Power?' I asked. 'If he's *The Times* correspondent I want to see him.'

Stewart said he'd go and fetch him and left the room.

'I suppose he's writing his despatch,' Herbin remarked, looking towards me, slightly maliciously.

'These journalist fellows simply amaze me,' De Coetlogon said. 'Scribble all day long, and never do a stroke of work. Not that I've got anything against the chap. At least he tells the truth—which is more than half of them do.'

'A week ago he sent a despatch to *The Times* saying the situation was desperate,' I said. 'Would you describe that as true?'

'Certainly,' De Coetlogon replied.

'You saw the townsfolk this morning,' I said. 'Would you describe them as—I quote—"only waiting for the Madhi to move before coming out against the Government"?'

'I believe that's the truth,' De Coetlogon replied. 'In any case it's the soldiers who defend this town—not the civilians.'

Herbin smiled. Then he gave me a look. It was a look of amusement; it was a look of complicity.

'But the civilians could in fact betray it,' Herbin said.

'Precisely,' De Coetlogon answered. 'So can the troops if they're disaffected, and these ones are.'

While he spoke Frank Power came in with Stewart. As soon as I saw Power my heart felt happier. I had been afraid he would be a sour-faced, embittered journalist of the type I had so often encountered. Instead I saw he was an eager, impetuous young man of about twenty-five. He had a pleasant expression and a fresh complexion. I sensed immediately that he was both intelligent and sensitive.

'General Gordon, I'm glad to meet you, sir,' he said coming up to me and shaking my hand. 'I tried to get through to you this morning, but the crowds were so thick I couldn't move. I was really afraid you would get squeezed to death. I've never seen such enthusiasm.'

'Have you reported that?' I asked.

'Of course I have,' the young man answered. 'It's the best story I've had for months. "Chinese Gordon"! They couldn't have sent for a better man. But I must confess, sir, I was a bit scared of meeting you after all the stuff I'd written.'

'You reported the truth,' De Coetlogon said, his jowls all aquiver. 'I'm sure General Gordon will appreciate the fact.'

'It was the truth then, all right,' Power replied.

'If it was the truth then, it's the truth now,' General De Coetlogon said.

It was when the man made that particular remark that I began to feel he was a defeatist.

'But don't you think the situation's rather changed?' Power asked him.

'I fail to see it,' De Coetlogon said flatly. 'The Mahdi's forces are still at El Obeid. Our line of retreat by land is closed by the Dervishes. Our line of retreat by river may well be closed by tomorrow.'

'I know all that, sir,' Power answered him. 'But I meant the situation here in Khartoum. A week ago half the Sudanese were just waiting for the chance to join the Mahdi. Now they're ready to fight him.'

'You change your opinions very rapidly, young man,' De Coetlogon said. He took out a bandana handkerchief and mopped his face.

'When situations change quickly, I hope I do,' Power answered. 'The General's arrival here has been worth a Division. Don't you agree, Herbin?'

Herbin smiled at me. Once again, when he spoke, his tone of voice was faintly malicious. But this time I could definitely feel that essentially he liked me.

'When I think of the huge swarms of Dervishes in the desert around us,' Herbin said. 'When I think of the embarrassment of having to choose between the Church and a fate, as you English say, far worse than death, I confess that a thousand redcoats would give me more confidence than the arrival of a British General, however great his charm.'

And he gave me a small bow.

I turned to young Power. 'Are you the man who cabled home a week ago to say that all talk of holding on to the town was bosh?' I asked.

'Yes, sir,' he replied stubbornly. With his curly hair and his rather snub nose he reminded me—at that moment—of an English schoolboy in the presence of the Head Prefect.

'Was it you who described the populace as a slumbering volcano?'

'Yes, sir.'

I laughed. 'What do you think now?' I asked.

'Your arrival has given the people who are against the Madhi a new lease of life,' Power replied.

'But you're not certain of the length of the lease, is that it?' I said.

As I spoke, Khalil, the Chief Cavass, came in, dressed in the full livery of a Palace servant. He bowed low to me.

'Ya Sidi . . .' he began.

Suddenly I recognized him. He was hugely built with a wide, fleshy face and an entrancing smile.

'Khalil, you rascal,' I said. 'Haven't they sacked you yet?'

Khalil rushed forward, knelt down and clasped my hand and kissed it.

'Get up, man,' I said. 'How are you?'

'Mabsut, ya Pasha, il hamdulillah!' he said.

'Have you forgotten your English?' I asked.

Khalil grinned. His teeth were very white. 'No, ya Pasha,' he said.

'Then go and bring us some drinks,' I told him. 'I'm sure these gentlemen are thirsty. Brandy for me—and lemonade for those who are wise enough to prefer it.'

'Hadir, ya Pasha,' my old friend said. Then he bowed low to the ground and went out.

'Now then, De Coetlogon,' I said, 'I want Stewart to hear your appreciation of our situation.'

'Would you like us to leave, Your Excellency?' Herbin asked tactfully. 'Mr Power and I can return later.'

'Certainly not,' I said. 'We'll probably be the only Europeans left in this town. If it falls we'll all be massacred together. You have every right to know how things stand.'

'I hope, General Gordon, that you won't take any of my remarks as a reflection on the reception you were given today,' De Coetlogon began. 'But the facts are these: thousands of people have arms hidden in their houses and are only waiting for the Mahdi to move before coming out against the Government. The bulk of the population is dispirited. They hate the Egyptians, and they fear the Mahdi.'

'What of the troops?' I asked.

'One-third of the garrison is unreliable,' De Coetlogon stated. 'The rest are incapable of holding off the Mahdi if he chooses to attack. We can hold out for another three weeks at the most. But if we leave *now* by river there's just time to escape to Berber. All the people with money have moved there already. I've got our fleet of river boats waiting with steam up on the Nile for your word to evacuate. I must tell you that I consider the situation is desperate.'

'Difficult,' I said. 'But not desperate.'

'You asked for my views,' De Coetlogon replied, sucking in his stomach as if he were on parade. 'I have given them.'

'Good,' I said. 'Now for plans. At dawn tomorrow the steamers must take away to Berber the sick, the wives and children of the Egyptian soldiers and civilian employees— as many as they can carry.' I turned to De Coetlogon. 'I'm told your wife is unwell,' I said. 'So I suggest that she could go with them. Then, in time we must evacuate every single Egyptian soldier.'

'The moment the troops leave there will be a revolt,' De Coetlogon answered.

'Precisely,' I said. 'Steps must be taken to prevent a state of anarchy arising on their withdrawal. Therefore, when I leave, first, I must be succeeded by someone who can control them. Zubair would be the right man—even though he was once a slaver. Secondly, that man must have behind him the moral support of *some* Government. At present the Egyptian Government is unfit to assume even a nominal responsibility for the Sudan. There is only one power that can undertake the duty. That country is England. And England *must* assume that responsibility until the day we have stamped out slavery and taught the people of the Sudan to govern themselves.'

Reading through these pages that I have written, I am aware at this point I may seem to have disregarded, quite arbitrarily, the orders which were given to me by the Cabinet. But in explanation I must state that my last instructions, contained in the sealed envelope, had been to comply with such orders or missions as I might be given by Sir Evelyn Baring in Cairo. And Baring felt that it was most unlikely that I should have been appointed Governor-General of the Sudan merely in order to carry out an inglorious retreat.

Further, he had not vetoed my plan to invoke the aid of Zubair to oust the Mahdi. Moreover, my reception that morning and my inspection of the troops later in the day had convinced me that my original assessment of the situation had been correct. Khartoum could be held.

I believed that in time the Mahdi's forces would crumble. And I now felt a burning conviction that it was England's duty to protect the Sudan until she was ready to govern herself.

However, General De Coetlogon scarcely troubled to conceal his contempt of my views.

'How long will your idealistic plan take?' De Coetlogon asked.

'Perhaps a hundred years,' I said.

'How long will it take you to persuade England to accept this responsibility?' De Coetlogon continued.

'I wrote out my report this afternoon,' I said. 'But knowing the Cabinet and Mr Gladstone, I should allow five weeks, perhaps even five months.'

'Khartoum can hold out against the Mahdi for another three weeks,' De Coetlogon stated. 'Not a day more.'

'There's no shortage of rifles and ammunition,' I pointed out.

'No,' said De Coetlogon. 'But there's a shortage of food.'

'Have you searched the granaries?' I asked. 'Have you

requisitioned the maize—their doura? I know these people. When we begin to requisition, you'll find that merchants like Bordeini have got enough food hidden away to last a year. If they haven't, we must send out armed foraging parties.'

For a moment there was silence. I could feel that Stewart was being influenced by De Coetlogon's arguments.

'Are you satisfied with the state of the defences?' De Coetlogon asked me.

'No,' I answered. 'I think we should put down mines.'

'There are no mines in the Arsenal,' De Coetlogon replied.

'Then we must make them,' I said. 'I've had to do that before now.'

'I thought we had been instructed to evacuate Khartoum,' De Coetlogon said.

'The instructions that I received in Cairo give me two objectives,' I explained. 'I must withdraw the Egyptian garrison and European civilians from Khartoum. I must also establish a form of Government to take over the administration of the Sudan as soon as the Egyptian troops have left. To do that I must remain in Khartoum. Those are my orders. And they've promised me they won't abandon us here.'

Power was looking out of the window. 'What's going on outside?' he asked. 'The crowds are thicker than ever.'

'Any excuse to celebrate,' De Coetlogon said. 'There'll be no more work done today, I can tell you that.'

'They've lit a bonfire,' said Power.

I walked over to Power and put an arm round his shoulder.

'If you want a spectacle to write about,' I told him, leading him out on to the verandah, 'come with me and you'll see a sight to gladden your heart. It's no ordinary bonfire, I promise you. During the last three hours I've had collected together every tax register, every whip and every lash. And now they will all be burned. The evidence of debts and the emblems of oppression will perish together.'

'Can I use that phrase in my despatch?' young Power asked eagerly.

I smiled. 'If you want to,' I replied.

De Coetlogon had joined us on the verandah. He stood holding his stomach in as usual, scowling down at the excited crowds.

'You seem displeased,' I said to him.

'I'm as revolted by flogging as any man,' De Coetlogon replied. 'But they've been used to the lash as long as they can remember. You can't keep discipline without it. We need to strengthen our authority, not weaken it.'

'My authority depends on their respect not on their fear,' I said.

'Why should the taxes be remitted?' De Coetlogon asked. 'Why should the treasury suffer?'

'Do you know how the money is collected?' I enquired. 'Have you seen the collectors at work? Do you know of their tortures? Look at the money that has come in already. Why do you think that so many of the coins are strung together? Because they're the ornaments the girls wear. They've been snatched from the necks of those too weak to resist.'

De Coetlogon turned impatiently away from his contemplation of the swarming crowds below.

'This town is surrounded by vast hordes of fanatics who would kill every single one of us without mercy,' he said. 'Our troops are untrained and unreliable. As Commander of the Garrison I must insist that this is a moment to increase discipline—not to relax it. We should continue to punish any men found guilty of indiscipline.'

'Punish—yes,' I answered. 'But let it be tempered with mercy and the knowledge that we deserve the same fate.'

'These people mistake leniency for weakness,' De Coetlogon stated. 'We're in Khartoum, General Gordon, not Kensington Gardens.'

'People respect kindness whether their faces are black or purple,' I said—perhaps rather tactlessly because it must have been obvious both to Power and to Herbin that, in his anger, De Coetlogon's face had turned a deep shade of mauve.

'I have come to help the people of the Sudan,' I continued. 'Not a handful of Pashas and despots who keep them in submission by fear and cruelty. The people are intelligent enough. I want them to learn to govern themselves.'

De Coetlogon swallowed. With his rather beaky nose and livid complexion he reminded me of a turkey-cock.

'Then let me confine myself to purely military matters,' he said. 'As Commander of the Garrison and a General of the Khedive's forces I have stated that Khartoum cannot hold out for more than three weeks.'

'I am convinced that Khartoum must and will hold out for another six months,' I replied. 'By which time the whole situation may have changed or the Cabinet may have reached a fresh decision.'

'I shall make my report in writing tonight,' De Coetlogon announced. 'If my advice is disregarded, I cannot hold myself responsible in any way for what may happen to those of you who choose to remain behind. But I intend to take such measures as I think fit to save the lives of the troops under my command.'

He gave a contemptuous look towards the bonfire and moved to go.

'One moment,' I said.

De Coetlogon stopped a few feet away from the door and turned found and faced me.

'You are Commander of the Garrison,' I told him. 'But as Governor-General I represent the Khedive of Egypt and the British Cabinet. I have authority to take decisions on the spot. I have told you my plans. I intend to see that they are carried out.'

'I can't accept your plans,' De Coetlogon stated.

In addition to Stewart, whose duty it was to listen to my words with De Coetlogon, I was very much aware that Power and Herbin were both listening intently to our conversation. I could easily have asked the two of them to go. But since their lives might depend on the outcome of the argument, I believed it was right that they should stay.

'You refuse to accept my plans?' I asked. I could feel that I in my turn was beginning to lose control of my temper.

'If you want to put it that way, yes,' De Coetlogon answered, his jowls quivering. 'I have my instructions from Cairo and I intend to obey them.'

I controlled my anger. I made myself remain perfectly calm. I cleared my mind. I took my decision. I spoke firmly but quietly.

'Then as Governor-General I must relieve you of your Command,' I said.

For a moment it seemed as if De Coetlogon had not heard my words.

'Can you be serious?' he asked after a pause.

'Perfectly,' I answered. 'You can leave with your wife on the steamer tomorrow.'

Then the import of my decision struck him. His face stiffened.

'You realise that I shall be forced to make a precise report of the causes of my . . . my resignation?' He was so angry that he had begun to stammer.

'You can report what you like,' I said.

'I can state that after being here barely seven hours you refused to accept the simple military factors as presented to you?' he asked.

'Certainly,' I replied.

'Have you any explanation for the War Office in London?' he asked.

'No,' I answered. 'But I have a message. Tell them that Khartoum is as safe as Kensington Gardens.'

Furious as he was, De Coetlogon still remembered to pull in his stomach as he stood erect and defiant before me.

'Goodbye, sir,' he said.

Then he inclined his body forward in what I suppose he

imagined to be a bow—and left the room. The noise of the crowd outside was growing louder. I turned to Herbin.

'The Europeans in the town will leave in the steamers tomorrow,' I told him. 'I would be delighted if you stayed. But, officially, as French Consul there is no reason now why you should not go. Would you like to accompany the General tomorrow? The steamers will leave before dawn. You must decide soon.'

'If you permit, I will stay in Khartoum for the moment,' Herbin answered. 'And if you will now excuse me I will go off to alert the Europeans for whom I am responsible. Good afternoon, Excellency. Thank you for your courtesy.'

I now turned to Power. His gentle brown eyes were gleaming with excitement.

'What about you?' I asked. 'Would you like to get out while you can? You've been here quite a time, Stewart tells me.'

Power's answer was enthusiastic and sincere. 'I want to stay here, sir,' he said. 'If I have the choice, I will not leave Khartoum until you do.'

'I hope you won't regret your decision,' I said. 'I think it will all end well if they don't betray me in Cairo and London.'

I noticed that Stewart had been oddly silent. 'What do you think, Stewart? What's your opinion?' I asked.

'At the end of seven hours I'm still confused, sir,' he replied.

I felt far more cheerful now that I had made my final decision. 'You'll soon get the hang of it,' I told him. 'And now De Coetlogon's gone there'll be all the more for you to do.'

'I've never been afraid of hard work, sir,' Stewart answered stolidly.

I laughed. 'I know,' I said. 'That's why I chose you. So I could slack now and then.'

Power was still standing on the verandah.

'The people are calling for you, sir,' he said.

Above the roar of the crowd I could hear the names 'Father' and 'Sultan'. I buttoned up the tunic of my white uniform before I stepped out on to the verandah. The din swelled as the crowd saw me. I raised my hands for silence. Then I spoke to them in their own tongue. I write down here the words I used.

'Geetkum bela' asakir bas all wa ragabte ashan akhallis al Sudan min al shar wa kulli shi kaa'b feehu. Wa a'na ma dayir aharib la beer nar wa la bee silah, bas bilhak wa al nisaf.'

I append a translation.

'I come without soldiers but with God on my side to redress the evils of the Sudan,' I said. 'I will not fight with any weapons but justice.'

If I had died that night, while the crowd roared its acclaim, I would have died a hero . . . But that moment has passed . . . Should I die tonight, nearly ten months later, I'd be known as a good soldier—I admit it. But they'd say I was unbalanced, tyrannical, impatient, stubborn . . . Perhaps they'd be right . . . With each day that passes, I can feel the heroism leaking out of me—leaking out with the petty problems of each day.

23 December

An Arab boy came in from the Mahdi's lines last night. He told us that the Mahdi puts pepper under his nails, and when he receives visitors then he touches his eyes and weeps copiously; that he eats a few grains of doura openly, but in the interior of the house he has fine feeding and enjoys alcoholic drinks.

After this, I think I shall drop any idea of writing the Mahdi letters, trying to convince or persuade him to reasonable measures. I must confess that the pepper business has sickened me; I had hitherto hoped I had to do with a regular fanatic, who believed in his mission. But when one comes to pepper in the fingernails, it is rather humiliating to have to succumb to him, and somehow I have the belief that I shall not have to do so. One cannot help being amused. Those who come in, for pardon, enter on their knees, with a halter round their neck. The Mahdi rises, having scratched his eyes and obtained a copious flow of tears, and takes off the halter! As the production of tears is generally considered the proof of sincerity, I would recommend the Mahdi's recipe to British Cabinet Ministers, justifying some job. The nails, I suppose, must be long in order to contain the pepper.

Christmas Day

I toss up in my mind, whether, if the place is taken, to blow up the Palace and all in it, or else to be taken, and, with God's help, to maintain the faith, and if necessary to suffer for it (which is most probable). The blowing up of the Palace is the simplest, while the other course means long and weary suffering and humiliation of all sorts. I think I shall elect for the last, not from fear of death, but because the former has more or less the taint of suicide, as it can do no good to any one, and is, in a way, taking things out of God's hands.

This is not a very cheerful entry for Christmas Day—but then I do not feel cheerful.

This evening I am nervous and restless. On my inspection of our defences I found it hard to control my temper. Faregh accompanied me. He is the Commander of my black troops in Khartoum. I strengthened the Garrison soon after my arrival by recruiting a number of volunteers and by forming a force of Negro troops, drawn largely from the former slaves of the Sudanese who had gone over to the Mahdi. Faregh is jet-black, tall, broad-shouldered and imposing. He can also be extremely stupid—as he was this evening.

I shall try to calm my irritated nerves by resuming my narrative of the events which have led me—and the people of Khartoum—into our present position.

By the middle of March this year our lines of communication with the outside world had been broken. The telegraph line had been cut, and I could send messages down the Nile only by courier.

I built two more steamers. I had eleven of them in all, and I armed each one of them.

I had found and trained a good man—Mohammed Ali Bey, who was beginning to show a brilliant ability for staging unexpected and minor attacks on the Mahdi's forces. I would, of course, have liked to have led these expeditions myself, but Stewart and the rest of them dissuaded me from doing so.

In mid-summer I began to plan a major attack down-river —on Berber. If we could take Berber our communications would be re-established, and the Mahdi's prestige would suffer. However, before I could send off such an expedition in my penny-steamers there was one task to be accomplished up-river. The Mahdi's most important followers, Sheik El Obeid and his sons, were encamped only twenty-five miles from us. (One constant confusion in the days when we could send telegraphs was the fact there existed El Obeid, the town, and Sheik El Obeid, the man, and poor Baring in Cairo always believed that I was trying to pursue a town.)

Early in September I sent off Mohammed Ali Bey for the Sheik's head-quarters. With him I sent a thousand men, and a flotilla of steamers. His attack was certainly successful. He destroyed the headquarters and defeated the Arab force.

I can only too easily recall the scene in my Operations Room next door to my bedroom on that late afternoon of 9 September. Frank Power had just come in to join the rest of us. The young man looked elated but—for some reason—a little worn. He had just written a despatch which he hoped to get smuggled down the Nile somehow by one of my spy-couriers.

'It's the first big victory we've had,' Frank said enthusiastically.

'Last night you were saying that Mohammed Ali wasn't the right man,' Stewart answered dourly.

Frank was silent. We all knew that Stewart himself had wanted to lead the expedition, but I had refused to let him go because a slight wound in his left arm had become badly infected.

'I must say that I think the moment has come when we should consider making new plans,' Stewart announced suddenly.

I swung round from the map I'd been examining.

'And do what?' I asked.

'Leave by the steamers and let the townspeople surrender to the Mahdi who will spare their lives,' Stewart replied in his usual dispirited voice.

'Surrender when we've just won a great victory?' I asked.

Herbin turned towards Stewart in exasperation. 'What makes you think the Mahdi will spare their lives?' he asked Stewart.

Stewart gave Herbin an odd look.

'I don't "*think*",' he answered. 'I know it. I also believe that Gladstone has been right in refusing to send an Expeditionary Force. What is the use of holding on to this country? They were savages when we came. They'll be savages when we leave, and probably much happier.'

Herbin smiled at him maliciously. 'But are we certain that your Prime Minister has decided *not* to send an Expeditionary Force?' he enquired.

Stewart glared at him.

'The last message from the Government, before the telegraph lines were cut, asked—I quote—"the cause and intention with which General Gordon continues at Khartoum",' Stewart replied stiffly, 'and—again I quote—"and instructed him to adopt at the first proper moment measures for his own removal". Does *that* sound as if they intended to send an Expeditionary Force?'

I decided the moment had come when I should intervene.

'The last message I received from Baring in Cairo instructed me to remain here,' I said.

Suddenly Herbin laughed. 'There!' he said with a chuckle. '*Now* do you see why every nation in Europe thinks that every plan of the British Government is positively Machiavellian? Why? Because your plans are completely incomprehensible to us. And why are they incomprehensible? Because you cannot even understand them yourselves. What is General Gordon doing here? Why was he sent? Your Prime Minister says one thing, your War Office another. What is he now to do? Go or stay? This time your Foreign Minister says one thing, and your Minister in Cairo says quite the opposite. To add to all the confusion, their messages arrive in the wrong order, and we have heard nothing since March when the telegraph lines were cut. Is there anyone in London or Cairo or Khartoum who understands your precise policy, your precise plan of action? No. Not one of you. Will even historians be able to pierce the fog, the British fog that has hung over this Sudan affair from the day it started? I doubt it. And yet, when your actions are determined by forces and methods so strange that you cannot even understand them yourselves, you blame us for thinking you Machiavellian. Perfide Albion! Poor Perfide Albion!'

I laughed. That evening for a while at least I was happy, and I felt that both Herbin and Power were my friends. I had already had misgivings about Stewart. I was well aware, by now, that he was more interested in his career than in relieving Khartoum. He was intensely ambitious. One evening in the Mess, when I had insisted that we must stay in Khartoum, he told us quite bluntly that he did not favour our staying because he did not like to be mixed up with a failure. It would be bad for his career, he explained. But at that moment I could forget my doubts about him.

'What do you think the General should do?' Frank Power asked Herbin. 'Obey Baring in Cairo and stay at his post, or take Gladstone's message as an order and go?'

Herbin smiled at me. There was no malice in that smile— only friendship, and, it seemed to me, a touch of pity.

'He must do the only thing he *can* do,' Herbin answered. 'Obey his own conscience.'

Herbin glanced towards Power and Stewart.

'You see, the General is not concerned with what Mr Gladstone or you and I think of his behaviour,' Herbin explained. 'He plays out his life before only one Person. Haven't you understood? He ignores the opinions of us poor mortals and relies only upon Almighty God. So what else can he do but act according to his conscience?'

'Is that what *you* will do?' I asked Herbin

'Oh no,' he answered. 'But remember I am a Frenchman.'

'Then what *will* you do?' Stewart asked bluntly.

Herbin smiled at him mischievously. 'Act according to my own interests,' he replied.

'But you're still here,' Frank Power said. 'You could have left ages ago.'

'I used to like the warm climate of Khartoum in Autumn,' Herbin answered. Then he lowered his voice and spoke in a whisper to Power. To this day I'm uncertain whether he intended me to hear what he said or not. Perhaps he didn't care either way—because I suspect that he had already made his decision to leave Khartoum.

'In addition,' Herbin said, 'but do not tell the General—I like warm girls with black skins. Also I do not share Colonel Stewart's fear of my reputation suffering if—as the Colonel once put it—"I should be mixed up in a failure".'

His voice resumed its normal tone. 'Besides I am certain the British Government will send troops,' he continued. 'I believe they meant to all along. If they were only honest enough to admit it to themselves—that is why they sent out the General.'

'I don't believe it for one moment,' Stewart said.

'Very well,' Herbin replied smoothly. 'Suppose they did not want to send out an expedition, they will be forced to now.'

Stewart's eyes flickered uneasily towards me. 'Why?' he asked.

Herbin looked at Frank Power and gave him a wink.

'Because of our young friend's last despatch before the lines were cut,' he replied. 'Let me quote—"We are daily expecting British troops," our dear friend said. "We cannot bring ourselves to believe that we are abandoned by the Government." I cannot imagine words better phrased to appeal to the sentimentality of the great British public.'

Khalil came in with a short despatch which I read quickly.

'With only a third of the Garrison we've routed the Sheik El Obeid and destroyed his forces,' I said. 'Mohammed Ali is still pursuing him. He'll be all right so long as he remembers my orders and never moves out of range of the steamers' guns.'

As I spoke there was a loud explosion on the Omdurman side of us. Frank Power started violently.

'I think you'd better pour yourself a brandy and soda,' I said to him. 'I'll have one, too. That was only one of our mines going up. Probably some poor wretched mule again. You're a bit jumpy tonight, Frank,' I added.

'It's nothing,' Power muttered as he crossed to the drinks-tray. When he handed me the drink, however, I observed that his hand was trembling. I pretended not to have noticed it.

'I must write a report tonight and try to smuggle it out by one of our men,' I said.

'I'd give anything to be able to telegraph a despatch tonight,' Power said. 'How I wish the Dervishes hadn't cut the lines.'

'I don't altogether agree with you,' I answered. 'At least I'm spared the annoyance of those telegraphs from London. Really—the pomposity of them! "Her Majesty's Government continues to be anxious to learn from General Gordon himself his views and position so that if danger has arisen or is likely to arise they may be in a position to take measures accordingly." What do they think is going on in Khartoum? A picnic? But I suppose I shouldn't blame them. How do I know if my last reports have got through? Every one of them may have been captured by the Dervishes.'

Stewart had strolled away from us and was examining the map.

'Did you manage to inspect our fort at Omdurman this morning?' I asked him.

'Yes,' he replied.

'Were they alert?'

'As alert as usual,' he answered.

As he spoke, Faregh, the Commander of the black troops, rushed in. He was sweating and distraught. He saluted me and stood in silence, staring at me. He was so agitated that he was for an instant speechless.

'What is it?' I asked. 'Speak, man!'

'Mohammed Ali Bey is killed,' Faregh blurted out.

I put my glass of brandy down on to the table. For all my concern, I was interested to observe that my hand was steady.

'And the men under him?' I asked.

'Killed,' Faregh answered. 'The Dervishes surround them from all sides. The Dervishes cut them into pieces.'

I tried to force my voice to sound calm.

'How many have escaped?' I asked.

'Less than two dozen men from the thousand,' Faregh replied.

'Where did the battle take place?' I asked.

'Twenty miles from the river,' he answered.

At that instant I could feel the waves of rage that I have experienced from my childhood surging through me. I could feel my heart pounding rapidly. For a few moments the whole room seemed blurred. I picked up my glass of brandy and gulped it down. But I had almost lost control. The waves were swirling in my head.

'I ordered Mohammed Ali not to go inland,' I shouted. 'I ordered him not to leave the protection of the steamers' cannons. The criminal fool! He's lost us a third of the Garrison.'

I strode to the windows and stood there trying to control myself. Vaguely I was aware that the conversation in the room was continuing.

'Have the townspeople heard the news?' Stewart asked Faregh.

'They will hear it,' Faregh answered. 'We cannot stop it.'

I walked back from the window. I knew that my hands were now trembling. I no longer cared.

'Stewart couldn't lead the expedition because he's wounded,' I told them. 'I wanted to go. Why did you persuade me against my own judgement?'

'Because you could not be spared from Khartoum,' Herbin replied quietly.

'We were afraid that you might be killed, sir,' Power added.

'Better a bullet in the head than to flicker out unheeded,' I said bitterly. I turned to Faregh, who was still standing by the door. 'Faregh,' I said, 'go back to your men. I want all troops on the alert tonight.'

'Should I go with him?' Stewart asked.

'No, stay here,' I said. 'We must make new plans.'

Faregh saluted me and went out. I poured myself another drink. The pounding of the waves had grown less. I turned to the three men in the room.

'We can now only hold out for three months at the most,' I said. 'If an Expeditionary Force does not reach us soon Khartoum will fall. I shall make one last appeal for Baring in Cairo to send to the Cabinet.'

'How can you be sure that your message will get through?' Herbin asked.

'There is only one way,' I answered. 'I shall send it on the steamer *Abbas*. Once past Berber, the river's more or less open.'

I paused. I looked slowly around the room.

'The steamer *Abbas* will leave before dawn tomorrow,' I said. I turned to Herbin. 'Your duties as French Consul ended some months ago, with the departure of the last of your fellow-countrymen,' I told him. 'But you have stayed on with us, and I'll always be grateful for the help and advice you've given us. I have a feeling that you would now like to leave us. Would you like to go off with the *Abbas* to-morrow?'

Herbin glanced at me. Then he stared down at the liqueur-glass in his hand.

'It might be a help if I were to deliver your report to the Minister in Cairo personally,' he replied.

'That's a good idea,' I answered. 'But I shall miss you.'

'I shall be sorry to leave for many reasons,' Herbin said. 'But I think the right moment has come.'

He looked at me and gave a rueful smile.

'For once I can say quite honestly, "It was a pleasure",'

he said. 'I hope we shall meet again. Now, if you will excuse me, I shall see to my affairs.'

I shook his hand. At the door, he paused.

'Please do not think me impertinent,' he said to me. 'But permit me one last word. I know that you act according to your conscience. But sometimes, just sometimes, remember your own interest. Goodbye, Excellency.'

Herbin gave me a little bow and went out quickly.

'Frank, could you write a despatch to *The Times* for Herbin to take with him?' I asked.

'Yes, sir,' he answered after a pause. Then he followed Herbin out of the room. I was left alone with Stewart. Once again he was examining the map. He looked more downcast than ever.

'Stewart, do you approve of sending down the *Abbas*?' I asked him.

'Yes,' he replied.

'You're very silent tonight,' I said. 'I hope your wound's not hurting you.'

'It's much better, thank you, sir,' Stewart answered in a voice without any expression.

I decided I must try to break the barriers of his reserve. 'There's something on your mind,' I said. 'What is it?'

Stewart turned and faced me. He spoke so deliberately that I'm sure he had worked out each word he had to utter.

'I think the time has come for you to leave Khartoum,' he said to me. 'I think you should leave tomorrow on the *Abbas*.'

I stared at him in complete astonishment. The idea he was proposing was—to my mind—as wilfully wrong as if he had suggested that I murdered Baring in Cairo.

'But I cannot leave Khartoum,' I explained. 'It would not be right. If I were to leave, the people could say this in just reproach to me: "You came up here. If you had not come some of us would have got away to Cairo. But we trusted in you and we stayed. We suffered and are suffering great privations in order to hold the town. Had you not come, we should have given in at once and obtained pardon. Now, as it is, we can expect no mercy from the Mahdi. He will avenge on us all the blood that has been spilt around Khartoum. You have taken our money and our food, and promised to repay us. All this goes for nothing if you leave us. No. It's your bounden duty to stay with us and share our fate. Because the British Government has deserted us, that is no reason for you to do so." '

'But the Mahdi will show the people mercy if they surrender,' Stewart said. 'I know it.'

'How can you know it?' I asked.

For one moment I saw a smirk of triumph on Stewart's face.

'Your former agent, Giuseppe Cuzzi, crossed our lines under a white flag two hours ago,' he announced 'He has brought a message from the Mahdi.'

'Why didn't you tell me?' I demanded.

'Because I knew that after your victory you'd pay no more attention to it than you've paid to the Mahdi's other messages,' Stewart replied.

'So you expected defeat?' I said.

'No,' Stewart replied. 'But I was waiting for a more suitable opportunity to discuss the whole position with you.'

'What was the Mahdi's message?' I asked.

Stewart quoted the Mahdi's words slowly, and almost reverently.

'If you will surrender Khartoum you will save yourself and all those under you,' he said.

'How can you believe such a promise when, in Berber, the Dervishes killed every single man, woman and child?' I asked.

'Will you at least see Giuseppe Cuzzi?' he enquired.

'I will not see my former agent,' I answered. 'I will not see Slatin, my former Commander at Darfur—nor any other Christian who has abjured his Faith to save his skin.'

'Then at least listen to my reasons why you should leave Khartoum,' Stewart urged. 'First, I don't agree that you owe these people a duty. They should consider themselves lucky that we came. Secondly, Faregh Pasha could be left in command . . .'

I interrupted him immediately. 'I declare positively once and for all that I will not leave the Sudan until everyone who wants to get away is given the chance to do so,' I said. 'Until then I shall stay here and fall with the town if it falls.'

'I am afraid it *will* fall,' Stewart declared.

'Then you want to leave?' I asked him.

Stewart looked embarrassed. He shifted a few paces on his long, ungainly legs.

'I can hardly leave if you stay,' he announced.

'Why not, if I say you can?' I asked.

Stewart's mouth tightened.

'You know what would be said in London,' he muttered.

'But you want to leave?' I persisted.

Stewart hesitated. He began to play with a ruler that was lying on the desk in front of the map.

'Yes,' he answered after a pause. 'If—if you will exonerate me from deserting you.'

I took a deep breath. I stared steadily at him. I knew that the moment of decision had come.

'You are not deserting me,' I said clearly. 'I think you will be useful in charge of the *Abbas*.'

Again Stewart hesitated. 'Will you write me an order to go, sir?' he asked.

'No,' I answered. 'I'm not afraid of the responsibility of sending you away. But I will not order you into danger when I'm not there myself. And the journey is obviously dangerous.'

'I have my career to think about,' Stewart said. 'Could you write me an official letter?'

'Certainly,' I replied. 'If you take down a letter, I will sign it.'

Stewart sat down at the desk and took up a pen.

' "Dear Stewart," ' I dictated. ' "The *Abbas* is going down the Nile tomorrow. You say you are willing to go in her if I think you can do so with honour. You can do little here, and if you go, you can help me by telegraphing my views in London." '

I looked towards him.

'Will that do?' I asked.

'Thank you, sir,' Stewart replied. He had regained his dour reserve. Once more he was the ambitious regular officer.

'I will give you orders for the journey later this evening,' I told him.

Stewart moved towards the door, then stopped.

'I hope you won't think any the worse of me for going?' he asked.

I tried to keep the irony from my voice.

'Don't worry,' I said. 'I'll give you a good report.'

Stewart bowed his head. Then he paused. When he now spoke there was a pathetic trace of apology in his tone.

'That will help me greatly,' he said. 'Thank you, sir. You see, I have still my career to think about,' he explained.

He turned and left the room.

I walked out on to the verandah. Almost mechanically I looked through the telescope. But there was no boat to be seen on the river. The croaking of the bull-frogs sounded quite loud.

I tried hard to sympathise with poor Stewart. I can understand ambition only too well. But thanks to Almighty God I know that ambition rightly fades. In the end, when we stand before the Throne it will make no difference if we have been successful kings or wretched guttersnipes.

I know that I have often failed in the ideals I set myself. But at least I have tried to avoid being impressed by temporal authority. I once refused the Royal Command of the Emperor of Abyssinia. On a smaller—and even more petty—scale, only a few weeks before I left England this time, I refused to dine with the Prince of Wales. In my heart, I know that all temporal things are, in truth, of no consequence. When I think of the persons that I know, I sigh because I realise that in a few years time—or even tomorrow—a piece of ground, six feet by two feet, will contain all that remains of Kings, Princes, Ambassadors, Generals, and—of course—of my own unworthy self.

I was deep in thought. I was scarcely aware that Khalil—surely one of the most beautiful specimens of the Lord's Creation—had come in with a taper and lighted the candles in the big lantern which hung above my desk. Vaguely I was aware that he had gone out. Vaguely I was aware that Frank Power had come into the room, and was standing beside me. I walked back from the verandah and sat down at the desk beneath the lantern.

'I've finished my despatch,' Frank said. 'If only it gets there. I think you'll be pleased with it.'

There was a tremor in his voice. I looked up at him. The young, enthusiastic schoolboy had vanished. In his place stood an almost haggard-looking man.

'Do you think you ought to sit there, sir,' he asked, 'with the snipers on the opposite bank?'

I smiled up at him. I tried to infuse confidence into that smile, but, as I watched his eyes, I realised I had failed.

'If a bullet's going to get me,' I said, 'it will get me wherever I am.'

As I spoke I was aware that the remark was trite.

'I wish I could feel the same,' Frank answered, and offered me a tin of cigarettes. When he held out a match to light my cigarette I saw that his hand was trembling once again.

I told Frank the news that both Herbin *and* Stewart were leaving Khartoum on the *Abbas* at dawn.

'Do you want to go with them?' I asked casually.

'Since the telegraph lines were cut, I haven't done much good here, have I?' Frank said.

'For what it's worth,' I answered, 'you're still the acting British Consul. But I asked you if you wanted to go.'

Frank crossed to the drinks-tray and poured himself a brandy. The rifle-fire was sounding louder.

'If I reached Cairo I could telegraph home a whole series of articles,' he said. 'Perhaps they would do some good.'

I was so tired that it was an effort to disguise my emotions.

'You can leave with them at dawn if you want to,' I said.

Frank took a long gulp of his drink. He tried to smile.

'Perhaps I should go,' he said. 'After all—as you said yourself—there's no more work for me to do as acting British Consul.'

I realised that I must do all I could to make our parting easy for him.

'True enough,' I said. 'But you've been a wonderful help to me when I was down in the dumps. I shall miss you, Frank.'

Frank stared down at his glass.

'I said I would stay here until the day you left,' he mumbled.

I smiled. 'We all say things at times we don't mean,' I said.

Frank's hands clutched his head, then fell to his sides.

'But I did mean it, sir,' he said in quiet desperation. 'I mean it still. I don't want to go. But I must.'

Slowly I got up from my desk and faced him.

'Why *must* you go?' I asked.

Suddenly—for the first time—Frank broke down.

'Can't you see?' he asked passionately. 'Can't you understand? Why do you have to make me tell you—when I've tried to keep it from you for so long? I wouldn't tell you now—except that I can't bear you to think I want to leave you. Can you still not understand? Why do you think I never go near the window at night? Because I can't bear it any longer. I can't sleep. I just lie there thinking of them all around us for hundreds and hundreds of miles . . . I see their dirty smocks. I see their long swords . . . I can smell the reek of their bodies . . . I can hear their screams as they break through the defences to mutilate us before they cut us to pieces. I can feel the thrust of their spears—into my body.'

I did not move—though I longed to pour myself another brandy. I decided that the only way I could help my dear friend was to be completely honest with him.

'You're not a soldier, Frank,' I said, 'and you're very young . . . It's over six months now since they surrounded us. All our nerves are on edge. I'm not afraid of death, but I'm very much afraid of defeat and its consequences. I don't believe a bit in the calm, unmoved man. Any loud noise in the air makes me jump. I'm horribly afraid of the Dervishes, though I have to pretend to be fearless, because I'm a soldier and in command. But you're not. I was selfish just now when I asked you why you must go. I suppose I didn't want to lose a good secretary. But there's every reason why you should go. Your articles in the papers will do far more good than my dull reports. You must go, Frank,' I concluded. 'I want you to.'

The rifle-fire had by now definitely grown louder.

'You've lost your nerve,' I continued. 'But you're not a coward. I can prove it to you.'

Suddenly, I spoke in a voice of complete authority.

'Sit down at that desk, Frank,' I said, 'and take down my last despatch to Cairo.'

Frank did not move.

'I'm waiting,' I said.

Frank hesitated. Then slowly he walked over to the desk and sat down under the lantern, in front of the open window. I stood close to the desk, looking down at him.

'Are you ready?' I asked.

'Yes, sir,' Frank said, almost inaudibly.

Slowly and deliberately I began to dictate what I realised might well be my last despatch. I felt, in a curious way, that even though Frank might not reach Cairo—even though my words might never be read by any living person—yet, since time and all the world are one, somehow my words might reach mankind.

'While you are eating and drinking and resting on good beds,' I dictated, 'we and those with us, both soldiers and servants, are watching by night and day, endeavouring to quell the movements of the false Mahdi . . .'

I paused. Frank looked up at me.

'Are you frightened?' I asked.

'No,' he answered.

'And you're sitting in the very centre of the one window they always aim for,' I said. 'That's not bad, is it?'

Frank tried to smile. 'I suppose not,' he answered.

As I continued my dictation I let my mind swing away from Frank Power. I had the strange sensation that I was unleashing an arrow that might never reach its target—yet might for ever stay in flight.

'You have been silent all this while and neglected us,' I dictated. 'If troops were sent, this rebellion would cease. It is, therefore, hoped that you will listen to all that is told you by Stewart and Herbin and Power, and look at it seriously and send us troops, as we have asked, without any delay.'

The *Abbas* left for Khartoum on 10 September.

I had planned the voyage down the Nile with the most meticulous care. I had, as far as I could, foreseen every conceivable danger. I had thought of every detail. I had arranged that two of the larger penny-steamers, the *Safia* and the *Mansura*, should escort the *Abbas* part of the way down the river. I had fitted the *Abbas* with buffers which stretched a foot under water to protect her from hidden rocks. And then, before they started, I took Stewart aside and warned him against landing to get wood—except in isolated spots—and I told him always to anchor in mid-stream. Yet I felt uneasy about the journey. I was afraid of Stewart's over-confidence in his own judgement. He was a man who did not think first, never thought of the prospective danger. Stewart was not a bit suspicious—while I am made up of doubts.

29 December

Little to report. I am rather in the dumps today. Why has the Expedition not yet arrived? Have they not had my letters? Did they not receive my journals? Do they not realise the urgency of my need?

I have despatched a runner with a message for the Expeditionary Force. I wrote it on a scrap of paper and sealed it with an Arab seal. The message was an act of defiance and bravado—something to wave in front of the Mahdi's face if my runner is intercepted. The message was brief. It read: 'Khartoum is all right. Could hold out for years!'—that should confound the Mahdi. Of course, there is always the chance the runner will get through to Wolesley—which would be just what I don't want to happen. The confounded Expeditionary Force moves with the speed of a tortoise. If this message reaches them, it is certain to slow them down even more.

It is strange how one becomes used to the shelling and sniping, and soon one thinks almost nothing of it. Today, whilst making my tour of inspection of the fortifications I felt something sting past me. I flicked my face and when I looked at my hand, saw a thin trace of blood. I had thought it had been an insect buzzing near me. It was an extraordinarily lucky escape, but it shows me again that my faith helps me. It proves to me that He wishes to preserve me.

Still no sign of the Expeditionary Force which the British Government has sent out for the relief of Khartoum. It would be ironic if the Expedition arrived too late. Sometimes I think it *will* be too late—after all the massive delays and the obstacles thrown in its path by Mr Gladstone. Mr Gladstone does not seem to like me. He certainly has made little attempt to study and evaluate the situation in the Sudan or my situation here in Khartoum. But what can an elderly diplomatist know of something he has not experienced? Mr Gladstone only has knowledge of the Sudan from second-hand sources.

There is little to do here—except by way of constant checking, defences, food, medical supplies, tours of the town, and the hospital. I have to appear buoyant and hopeful at all times. I must not appear to be distressed. I must not feel alone or low. If I let my endeavour slacken for even a minute the soldiers and the townspeople will notice it and lose heart. That, I know, would be fatal. It is my resolve which holds this town against the Mahdi.

Even the most distressing moments, the most drastic setbacks have to be taken lightly.

In the last week of September one of my spies came in with the most ghastly news. He had been given first-hand information—from a usually reliable source—of the terrible fate of the *Abbas*.

The *Abbas*, he was told, with the forty men on board, partly European and partly Egyptian, besides five Negroes and three servants, arrived near the village of Salamat, where she ran aground, but did not founder.

Several persons from the steamer went ashore in order to reassure the natives, declaring that they had not come to make war, but to purchase camels in order to cross the desert to Merawi.

The Sheiks Soliman and Abu Noman, and the uncle of Faki Osman, agreed to see to their conveyance, and provided a guide, who was to conduct the party. Those on board the *Abbas* were so pleased with this attention that they presented one of the Sheiks with a gold sword, the uncle with a silver sword and the guide with a rich dress. Whereupon the Sheiks requested them to leave the steamer and accept their hospitality until preparations had been completed for crossing the desert. The invitation was accepted, and the party entered a house.

There they were all massacred—Frank Power, Herbin, Stewart—all of them.

The Sheiks afterwards returned to the steamer and killed most of those still on board. Of forty persons only fourteen were spared, and these were taken as prisoners.

I cannot get out of my head the *Abbas* catastrophe. That the *Abbas* (with her 970 bullet marks on her, with her gun and her parapets, which were bullet proof), could be captured by force still seems to me to be impossible. That she should run upon a rock seems so unlikely, for I had her sides defended by buffers, sunk one foot in water. I had warned them against ever anchoring by the river-bank. I had instructed them to take wood from isolated spots. In fact, as far as human foresight goes, I did everything possible to protect them.

It was not long after I had this distressing news about Stewart and Herbin and Frank Power that a messenger brought me a letter from the Mahdi.

I now transcribe it here:

'In the name of God the merciful and compassionate: praise be to God, the bountiful Ruler, and blessing on our lord Mahomed with peace.

'From the servant who trusts in God—Mahomed the son of Abdallah.

'To Gordon Pasha of Khartoum: may God guide him into the path of virtue, amen!

'Know that your small steamer, named *Abbas*—which you sent with the intention of forwarding your news to Cairo, by way of Dongola, the persons sent being your representative Stewart Pasha and the two Consuls, French and English, with other persons, has been captured by the will of God.

'Those who believed in us as the Mahdi, and surrendered, have been delivered; and those who did not were destroyed —as your representative afore-named, with the Consuls and the rest—whose souls God has condemned to the fire and to eternal misery.

'That steamer and all that was in it have fallen prey to the Moslems, and we have taken knowledge of all the letters and telegraphs which were in it, in Arabic and in Frankish, and of those maps, which were opened to us and translated by those on whom God has bestowed His gifts, and has enlightened their hearts with faith, and the benefits of willing submission. All has been seized, and the contents are known. It should all have been returned to you, not being wanted here, but as it was originally sent from you, and is known unto you, we prefer to send you part of the contents and mention the property therein, so that you may be certified; and in order that the truth may make a lasting impression on thy mind—in the hope that God may guide thee to the faith of Islam, and to surrender; that you and your followers may surrender to Him and to us, that so you and they may obtain everlasting good and happiness.

'Now . . . amongst the documents seized is the telegraph sent to the Khedive of Egypt and to the English Consul-General. Further, there is the letter found with the French Consul, written by you to him on 12 July 1884, No. 512/38, in acknowledgement of the 100 francs distributed to the poor and needy.

'Also your letters, written in European languages, all

about the siege of Khartoum, and all about the arranging of the steamers, with the number of the troops in them, and their arms, and the cannon, and about the movements of the troops, and the defeat of your people, and your request for reinforcements, even if only a single regiment, and all about how your agent Cuzzi turned Moslem.

'Also you refer to the useless waste of time, so much so, that from your repeated promises to the people of Khartoum about arrival of reinforcements, you have appeared to them as if you were a liar . . .

'We never miss any of your news, nor what is in your innermost thoughts, and about the strength and support—not of God—on which you rely. We have now understood it all.

'Tricks in making ciphers, and using so many languages, are of no avail.

'From the Most High God, to whom be praise, no secrets can be hidden.

'As to your expecting reinforcements, reliance for succour on others than God, that will bring you nothing but destruction, and cause you to fall into utmost danger in this world and the next.

'No doubt you have heard what has happened to your brethren, from whom you expected help, at Suakin and elsewhere, whom God has destroyed, and dispersed and abandoned.

'Notwithstanding all this, we have now arrived at Mushra'el Koweh', at a day's journey from Omdurman, and are coming, please God, to your place. If you return to the Most High God, and become a Moslem, and surrender to His order and that of His Prophet, and believe in us as the Mahdi, send us a message from thee, and from those with thee, after laying down your arms and giving up the thought of fighting, so that I may send you one with safe conduct, by which you will obtain assurance of benefit of the blessing in this world and the next. Otherwise, and if you do not act thus, you will have to encounter war from God and His Prophet. And know that the Most High God is mighty able for thy destruction, as He has destroyed others before thee, who were much stronger than thou, and more numerous.

'And you, and your children and your property, will be for a prey to the Moslems, and you will repent when repentance will not avail. For, after the beginning of the battle were you to surrender, it would be from fear, and not willingly, and that will not be accepted.

'And there is no succour or strength but in God, and peace be upon those who have followed the Guidance.

'Dated Wednesday 7th day of Moharram, 1302.

'22 October 1884.

'(Seal)   There is no God but (God) ALLAH
          'Mahomed is the prophet of (God) ALLAH
          'Mahomed the Mahdi (son of) ABD-ALLAH
                            (Year) 1292.'

This Seal was square, and very large. It was roughly engraved, and the inscription formed a triplet, each line ending with the name of God.

The letter was all written on one side of a very large sheet of paper.

5 January

There is no sign of the Expeditionary force. The troops should have been here by 20 December. According to a message smuggled through from Wolseley the Expedition were to begin the final leg of their march on 15 December; it should have taken them only five days to reach us. My promises to the people of Khartoum have no sting in them any more. They have all been made too often. The troops and the townspeople do not, as yet, disbelieve me, but it will come to that. They cannot be expected to have faith for so long with no sign of reward. They are a simple people, with only a childlike cunning, and only a child's faith and trust— they expect a promise to be fulfilled quickly and when it has to be reiterated they begin to doubt.

Our situation is desperate. Food is critically short in Khartoum. There's hardly any grain left. The supply of biscuits is almost exhausted. The inhabitants are reduced to eating horses, donkeys, dogs, rats and the gum from the trees. Any living beast which stirs runs the risk of being eaten. Dysentry is rife. Many of my Garrison are too debilitated by sickness and starvation to take their place in the lines. Soldiers frequently desert their posts to go searching for food. I doubt whether they find any.

Corpses fill the streets. Many of them are not moved from the place they fell. They are rotten and stinking and filled with disease. It is a wonder to me that we have not yet been infected by a plague. This interminable dry heat encourages it. I thank God that the heat is not as intensive now as in the Summer months. What can be done about these corpses? It would appear nothing. No one has the energy to bury them; no one cares.

We have been besieged here now for 296 days. I pray to Him there will not be many more. We have not been great heroes, but heroes we have been and the siege of Khartoum has been as good as that of Sebastopol. I fear that the town cannot survive much longer. If the Expeditionary Force does not come soon this town *may fall*.

I have always been aware that I am made up from two distinctly contradictory selves. Now I am conscious of having *become* two distinct beings. One of these selves toils ceaselessly and, I admit, sometimes impatiently, at a seemingly hopeless task. The other dwells calmly upon the eternal. I am learning—slowly—to be content in whatever state I am in. Thoughts have deepened in me, but nothing new. I ponder much upon the incidents of my life, and my purpose here in Khartoum.

We have had in detail nothing but disaster on disaster, yet in general we are successful. God will not let this solution give any glory to man. I have always felt that if we got through, it would be a scramble. There would be no glory to man. Our deliverance (if it happens) is due to the prayer of others. He is not unfaithful if we fall. For our destruction may be for His greater glory, and He does not promise to grant us everything we ask, if it is not good for us to have it. This may all be part of His great plan—it may be that our destruction is the seed of the fall of the Mahdi—and out of all this may come some good for the people of the Sudan. No matter. I am content. He will enable me to keep my faith and not deny Him—whatever may come.

In Fort Omdurman the situation has been utterly desperate for some days. The Garrison is starving and it is running short of ammunition. The Mahdi is attacking Omdurman as a prelude to launching his final attack on this town.

From the large telescope I have put on the roof I have watched the pathetic last spasms of my little fort at Omdurman, just across the river.

This afternoon their commander sent me a flag-signal to say that his men had run out of food and ammunition.

There was nothing I could do. With immense sadness and regret, mingling with a terrible foreboding, I signalled back the order for the Garrison in Omdurman to surrender.

The fall of Omdurman has made our position in Khartoum still more dangerous. It is only a matter of time before the Mahdi turns his full attention and all his forces on to us here.

6 January

This morning I issued a proclamation. I realise that it is essential to reduce the non-combatant element of the population. Because, by so doing, I shall reduce the number of mouths I have to feed. This may assist in making the small quantities of food go further, thus enabling us to hold out here for a while longer. This morning, therefore, I made a public proclamation in which I stated that any of the townspeople wishing to leave Khartoum may do so. I also sent a letter to the Mahdi asking him to feed and deal kindly with those who have left. None of the civil population can do us any harm by carrying details to the Mahdi of our defences and fortifications.

There is still no sign of the Expeditionary Force—why do they delay in coming?

7 January

Two slaves came in today; they say that the enemy lacks ammunition. I do not wonder at it, because of the way they fire away.

The Dervishes came down to the ruined village opposite and fired on the Palace all morning. I have got so accustomed now to the perpetual sound of firing that I can tell where the report is coming from—from the Dervishes on us or from my men on to the Dervishes.

A curious thing happened at the beginning of November when my friend Kitchener, who is with the Expeditionary Force, sent up one of his courier-spies to me with information—little of it new to me. He had wrapped up some letters in some old newspapers which were thrown out in the garden; there, a clerk, who knew some English, found them blowing about. He gave them to the apothecary of the hospital, who knows English. The doctor found him reading them, saw the date *15 September*, and secured them for me. They were like gold, as can be imagined, since we had had no news *direct* from England since 24 February 1884.

Did Kitchener send them by accident or on purpose?

'Lord Wolseley seen off at Victoria Station for the Gordon Relief Expedition!' No! I wish it had not been called the *Gordon* Relief Expedition. For it has come to relieve Khartoum and not me.

8 January

This morning, I was studying the map of our defences in a rather desultory fashion when Khalil, the Chief Cavass, came in, cleared his throat so that I should become aware of his presence, and gave me a deep bow. He is, I think, one of the most beautiful persons I have ever seen.

'Min fadlak, ya sidi,' he began shyly. 'I work hard for you for eleven months, Malik Gordon, yes?'

Immediately I knew that he had come to ask for some favour or the other.

'You've worked for eleven months,' I said cautiously.

'But I work hard,' Khalil insisted.

'Sometimes,' I said.

'I want to ask something,' Khalil told me. 'I want to ask big favour.'

'What is it?' I asked.

'Tomorrow I want leave to stay in my home all the day and night,' Khalil told me.

I enquired why.

'I want to marry,' Khalil announced.

'But you got married only five months ago,' I said.

Khalil grinned happily.

'Aiwa,' he agreed. 'But this is a new wife. I love her. I love her very much.'

Khalil has such a beguiling way with him that I find it hard to refuse his requests.

'All right, Khalil,' I said. 'Tomorrow all day and night. But not an hour longer,' I said.

'Ashkurak, ya sidi,' Khalil said, beaming happily. 'Thank you.'

Then he began a process of work which I am sure he considers to be 'tidying up'. This process consists in lifting up any book or ornament he can find lying around, blowing on it heavily, and then putting it back exactly on the spot where it came from. For a man of his height he moves with remarkable delicacy.

Suddenly I heard the sound of women wailing outside the Palace.

'What's that?' I asked Khalil. 'Why are the women screaming?'

'Perhaps it's a funeral,' Khalil said uneasily.

'I don't think so,' I said. 'Go out on to the balcony and find out.'

Khalil stopped his 'tidying up' and disappeared through the French windows. A few moments later he came back into the room.

'It is some of the women, ya pasha,' he said, looking down at his large black feet as he always does when he is embarrassed.

'They are crying to you for help, ya pasha,' he announced.

'What do they want?' I asked.

'Food,' Khalil replied. 'They have no food.'

I had already realised that our reserves were getting dangerously low. I had tried to buy more food from the various merchants in the town. But they had all apologised, and twisted and turned. And in the end they had wriggled out of it, and I had got nothing. But there was still one merchant I had left until last. He was a Sudanese of Syrian extraction called Bordeini. I had known the old rascal for years. I was certain he would have food stored away in some place where we'd never find it. But I had to discover a way to persuade him to produce it. Bordeini is the biggest merchant in Khartoum, and if I could persuade him then perhaps the others would follow.

An hour later Bordeini was shown into my room by Khalil. I gestured for him to sit in the most comfortable armchair. Bordeini is almost monstrously fat and rich. He is about fifty years old, affable and dishonest, yet completely capable of laughing at himself. He is a rogue, but a pleasant one, and he has a certain dignity.

He waddled in, beaming. 'The blessing of Allah be upon you, General Gordon,' he said, employing the usual ritual of greeting.

'And on you, Bordeini,' I answered.

'I hope your Excellency is in good health?' Bordeini asked, adding the conventional gambit.

'Thanks be to God,' I answered automatically. 'I am in excellent health. I trust that you too are in good health, Bordeini?'

'Praise be to Allah, I am still in good health,' Bordeini stated.

'Well, now we've got all that over,' I said briskly, 'how much food have you got in your store?'

Bordeini stared at me reproachfully. 'Excellency, you surprise me,' he said. 'You are too sudden.'

I smiled at him. 'Of course,' I said. 'I forgot. I should have offered you refreshment.'

Bordeini revealed several gold teeth as he grinned back at me.

'That is our custom,' he said.

'A glass of lemonade?' I asked.

·Bordeini looked down at the carpet and didn't reply.

'Oh, Bordeini,' I said, 'can it be that you would like something stronger?'

Solemnly Bordeini nodded his head.

'Beer?' I asked.

Bordeini remained silent.

'Brandy?' I enquired.

Bordeini nodded his head enthusiastically.

'Oh, Bordeini,' I said, 'and you a strict Mohammedan . . . Help yourself.'

'Allah will forgive me tonight,' Bordeini said as he crossed over to the drinks-tray.

'Why should he?' I asked.

'Because a great Englishman will ask for food I have not got,' Bordeini answered, watching me slyly. 'And when I say "no" he will be very angry, and I shall be very much afraid,' he added. Suddenly he looked at me. 'I trust her Excellency, your sister, is well?' he asked.

'Praise be to God when I last heard from her she was very well,' I answered automatically. 'Now, don't let's start all that business over again,' I continued. 'Bordeini, how much food have you got in your stores?'

'In my stores?' Bordeini asked innocently.

'In your stores, in your granaries, in your houses,' I said. 'How much doura? How much maize?'

'Perhaps one hundred ardebs,' Bordeini replied. 'One hundred bushels.'

'And biscuits?' I continued.

'Perhaps twenty thousand okes,' Bordeini answered nervously. 'Sixty thousand pounds in weight.'

'It's not enough,' I said.

'That is what I am saying. It is not enough,' Bordeini replied quickly. 'I have servants to feed and horses to feed and three wives to feed.'

'I thought you only had two wives,' I said.

Bordeini smirked complacently. 'Yes, I had two wives,'

he replied. 'But last week I marry another one. Very young, very nice.'

'And you've only got one hundred ardebs of doura and twenty thousand okes of biscuits?' I asked.

'Perhaps. Not more,' was the reply.

'That's bad,' I said.

'Yes, very bad,' Bordeini answered.

'It is less than a week's supply for the town,' I said. 'And you have many enemies.'

Bordeini took a swig of brandy.

'No, Excellency,' he answered. 'I am a good man.'

'Enemies who might tell me where your grain is hidden,' I continued firmly.

'Not possibly,' Bordeini said, without thinking. 'No man could.'

'So you have got grain hidden away,' I said.

'No,' Bordeini said hastily. 'Not one ardeb.'

'If I found you had a hidden store I might be very angry,' I announced. 'I might be so angry that I would put you in prison. And then you might not see your nice young wife for many months.'

Bordeini clasped his plump hands together.

'Excellency, do not say such things,' he pleaded, 'even in a joke.'

'But of course there's no question of it,' I said.

'Of course not, Excellency,' Bordeini said, looking obviously relieved.

'Because I'm sure you're only too willing to sell me some biscuits and doura at the current prices,' I said.

Bordeini's plump hands fluttered around his stomach worriedly.

'A little, certainly,' he said.

'And the figures you gave me just now apply only to your private store,' I said. 'So I would like to buy from you— shall we say six hundred ardebs of doura and one hundred and twenty thousand okes of biscuits?'

'I have not so much in all Khartoum,' Bordeini answered, almost tearfully.

'And I thought Bordeini Bey was the greatest merchant in all Khartoum,' I said in a voice of great sadness.

'Excellency, you said Bordeini *Bey*,' the man said.

'Did I? I must have been dreaming,' I replied negligently. 'As you know, I only bestow the title of Bey on men who have really done something towards the public good. Men who have really helped the people of the town to resist against the Mahdi. Soldiers who've fought well—like Faregh. Merchants who've sold food at some personal sacrifice . . .'

'Merchants too?' Bordeini asked, his hands now fluttering wildly with excitement.

'Why not, if they have helped the common cause?' I said. 'But now I come to think of it I *haven't* made a merchant a Bey yet. Of course, if a merchant *did* come forward to help me, I wouldn't hesitate. I'd make him a Bey there and then.'

Bordeini sank back into the large armchair. His forehead was glistening with sweat.

'Would it wrong your hospitality if I asked for another brandy?' he asked.

'Help yourself, Bordeini,' I said.

Bordeini levered himself out of the armchair and wobbled towards the drinks-tray.

'Did your Excellency say he wished to buy four hundred ardebs?' Bordeini asked, as he poured himself a large brandy.

'No,' I answered firmly. 'Six hundred ardebs of doura and one hundred and twenty thousand okes of biscuits.'

Bordeini sighed.

'It will be very difficult to find,' he said.

'Very difficult, I!' I agreed.

'It will be a great personal sacrifice,' Bordeini added hopefully.

'I'm certain of it,' I replied.

Bordeini took in a deep breath. His nervous hands were smoothing the folds of his robes into position.

'Then I will come forward to help you, Excellency,' he announced. 'I will find the food you asked for.'

I got up from my chair and crossed to my desk. Quickly I wrote out a directive, while Bordeini watched me anxiously.

'I have come forward,' Bordeini reminded me. 'I have helped the people's good.'

'I know it,' I replied. 'I'm most grateful to you Bordeini Bey,' and I handed him the document of his appointment as Bey.

Bordeini glanced at the sheet of paper, then clasped my hands.

'Thank you, thank you very much, Excellency,' he said, beaming excitedly. 'Excuse me, but I must go home. I have news . . .' he stammered. 'I have important work to do. Forgive me to say goodbye. Excuse me. Thank you, Excellency, thank you.'

He was almost incoherent with joy. Hurriedly he stumbled from the room.

Bordeini is dishonest, but he has always been strictly upright in his dealings with me. Late this afternoon he fully produced the food from his hidden stores. I summoned Faregh and instructed him to announce to the entire populace that for the next month there would be an increase in rations.

9 January

This afternoon Faregh came in with a letter which had been sent to me, under a white flag, by the Mahdi.

I transcribe the letter here:

'To Gordon Pasha, may God protect him,' the letter began, and after praising such good points as I might have, it went on to say: 'We have written to you to go back to your country . . . I repeat to you the words of God, "Do not destroy yourselves. God Himself is merciful unto you." I understand that the English are willing to ransom you alone from us for £20,000 . . . If you agree to join us it will be a blessing to you. But if you wish to rejoin the English, we will send you back to them without asking for so much as a farthing.'

'The three men under the white flag also bring you this,' Faregh said, and handed me a small bundle that he had been carrying.

I ripped open the bundle. It contained a slip of paper and some filthy, patched Dervish clothes. I flung the Dervish clothes away from me disgustedly. I kicked them aside as if they were contaminated.

Khalil, who was doing a little 'tidying up', gave a gasp of horror.

I smoothed out the slip of paper. It was another message from the Mahdi.

I translate it here.

'If you will deliver yourself up and become a follower of the true religion,' the Mahdi wrote, 'you will save yourself. Otherwise you shall perish.'

I turned to Faregh.

'Let the messengers be told that I do not deign to reply,' I said.

I have had letters, during these last few months, from Rudolf Slatin, and other Europeans who have been captured by the Mahdi. He has spared their lives on the condition that they adopt the Moslem faith.

I am told the Mahdi has provided these men with girls to live with them. I hear that my former agent, Giuseppe Cuzzi, has now adopted the Moslem name of Mohammed

Yusef, and that Slatin's Moslem name is Abdel Kadi. The Mahdi takes Slatin and all the Europeans with him when he moves.

When Slatin wrote to me, telling me that he wished to escape from his captors, and join me in Khartoum, I declined to be a party to his breaking his parole to the Mahdi. I did not consider him even worthy to receive the courtesy of a reply.

I try to make myself have charitable thoughts towards these men who have abjured their religion and their country in order to save their wretched skins. But, alas, I can only feel the most profound loathing and contempt for them.

10 January

In blackest bitterness of soul I continue to make my daily rounds. I talk with the town notables, observing all of the calm rituals, trying to convince them that the Relief Expedition is on its way and they have only got to hold out for another fortnight. But I can see from their eyes that, however much they may pretend, they do not really believe me. Their eyes are like the eyes of hurt, disappointed children.

I walk through the dusty, stinking streets of the town. I nod and smile at the people. I stop and talk with them. I try to encourage and cheer them. They are pitiful. They are all near starvation, generally depressed and ill. They know how much they stand to lose if the Relief Expedition does not come. And the ordinary people, unlike the notables, do not have anything to bargain with. They have stayed with me and—by so doing—they have openly defied the Mahdi. These simple townspeople know that if the town falls the Mahdi will not show them any mercy.

As I walk around the town I have to step aside to avoid the decaying corpses. I hold my breath to avoid breathing in the stench of putrefaction. How little man is when compared to His infinite wisdom. The only sounds are the sounds of the Dervish snipers and the moans of the sick. Otherwise Khartoum is strangely silent. Perhaps the silence is not so strange, for we have killed and eaten every natural thing. Now even the sparrows seem to avoid the town.

I walk around the four miles of the defences, trying to enhearten my soldiers, who stand like blocks of wood, staring out—with almost unseeing eyes—at the pitched tents of the Mahdi's camp. I try to enthuse them with confidence that the English Redcoats are on their way and that at any moment their trials will be over. My soldiers constantly abandon their posts, however, to go and forage for food. Starvation and dysentry make them a pitiable force. The mortality rate rises daily.

After doing my rounds of the defences I come back to the Palace. Here I sit, drinking a glass or two of brandy. This steels me to visit the hospital in which more than a hundred of my men—despite the slight increase in their rations—are dying each day. The hospital is appalling. In this foetid heat the stink is foul. It takes a great effort of will to breath the air in there, and the conditions are hopeless. There are no medical supplies. There have not been any for some time. Any kind of medical treatment is hastily improvised; it is a miracle if any man survives it. The men cry out to me to help them. They beg to know when the Redcoats are arriving. I try to encourage them—sometimes wondering if it is fair on them to raise false hopes. The hospital is appalling and pitiable. It twists my heart every time I visit the place.

An escaped soldier came in from the Dervishes—but with no news. He was so dreadfully itchy, I could not keep my patience, or keep him in my room. He saw himself in the mirror, and asked who it was; he said he did not know! And really he did not seem to know. It stands to reason that in countries where there are no mirrors, everyone must be a complete stranger to himself, and would need an introduction.

The sniping and shelling from the Dervishes are increasing each day as their forces and supplies increase. Each night I find it more difficult to sleep.

However, I have done what I can, and I can do no more than trust now. What has been the painful position for me is that there is not one person on whom I can rely; also, there is not one person who considers that he ought to do anything except his routine duty. We have now been blockaded for nearly a year, and things here are critical; yet not one of my subordinates, except the chief clerk and his subordinates, appears today. I had to send for them, and wait until they came for perhaps an hour.

'It is Friday, and it is unreasonable to expect us at the office,' is what they say.

My patience is almost used up with this apparently never-ending trial. There is not one department which I have not to superintend as closely as if I were its direct head. The officer who commanded the post, from which the men deserted, never told me about it, but he says he told Faregh Pasha. This Faregh Pasha denies, and so it goes on—with tissues of lies, and they no more care about being found out. It is indeed hopeless work, and yet, truly, they have been treated most handsomely in every way. Nearly every order, except when it is for their interest, has to be repeated two, or even three times. I may honestly say I am weary of my life; day and night, night and day, it is one continual worry.

My mission here was a special one, and not obligatory, like a military duty. In my position of Governor-General I am quite justified in having said and done everything for the people over whom I am placed.

A very little boy, with large, black, limpid eyes, came in from the Arabs. He had been captured some months ago. He is a smart lad. His name is Awaad and we have set him to work about the Palace.

11 January

In my last despatches I continually urged Baring in Cairo and the Government in London to send me Zubair— because I was convinced that Zubair and I together could settle the Mahdi's hash once and for all. But, though, for once, Baring supported me, the Cabinet would have none of it. They protested that the great British public would object to my using a notorious slaver. What do they know about it? They are not here and cannot understand the best methods. I venture to think that any attempt to settle this Sudan affair in the light of the emotions expressed in the British Press and by the British populace is sure to be productive of harm. In this, as in so many other cases, it would be sensible to follow the advice of the various authorities on the spot, and *not* of a collection of emotional old ladies in England.

Little Awaad is an assistant to Khalil. As I watched him scampering happily around the Palace this morning, I suddenly remembered that it was boys and girls of about nine and ten that Zubair in his great slave-trading days delighted to capture.

I remember a coffle of slaves I had once seen captured when I was out here six years ago. The Arab slave-dealer's had not even spared the youngest children from their assaults. There was a little girl—she can have been no more than nine—who was slowly bleeding to death from an internal haemorrhage as a result of having been raped by a dozen of them.

I found a tent for the child; I did all I could to try to stop the bleeding; I tried to comfort her and to relieve her pain. But life was slowly ebbing away from her. I shall never forget the look of anguish and bewilderment in her large dark brown eyes. Although I had made one of my female servants wash the girl frequently the blood continued to trickle down her thighs. And the flies were swarming in it.

She died on the second night. God had taken her into His merciful arms. I was no longer sorry for the little girl—because I knew she had found eternal peace and security.

12 January

One tumbles at 3 a.m. into a troubled sleep; a drum beats—tup! tup! tup! It comes into a dream, but after a few moments one becomes more awake, and it is revealed to the brain that *one is in Khartoum*. The next query is, where is this tup, tupping going on? A hope arises it will die away. No, it goes on, and increases in intensity. The thought strikes one, 'Have they enough ammunition?' (The excuse of bad soldiers.) One exerts oneself. At last, it is no use. Up one must get, and go on to the roof of the Palace; then orders, swearing, and cursing goes on. Men may say what they like about glorious war, but to me it is a horrible nuisance. (If it is permitted to say anything is a nuisance which comes on us.)

Last night I came back to bed at 4 a.m., after a visit to the Palace roof. Presently I fell into a fitful sleep.

I had the most vile nightmare of my life.

I was watching a coffle of about fifty slaves being driven across an expanse of open desert by half a dozen Arab traders. I was riding on a camel—as I used to in my days in the Equatorial Province. But for some reason I could not speak—nor could I even change the direction of my camel. I seemed utterly powerless to alter any of the circumstances or events that were taking place. Dimly, I was conscious of the camel's awkward gait. I was also aware that neither the slavers or the slaves could see me.

A small child from the coffle fell and lay motionless on the ground. It was a tiny girl. A trader came up to her and kicked her. She did not stir. He casually shrugged his shoulders, left her where she was and rejoined the coffle.

Overhead, the vultures wheeled and cried in the slowly darkening sky.

My camel had also rejoined the coffle. As I looked down from my saddle, I could see the strained, exhausted faces of the slaves.

Then—to my horror—I saw that one of the slaves was Awaad, the slim ten-year-old Arab boy who had come into our lines two days before, and whom I had installed as a servant in the Palace. I tried to move my camel towards him. My idea was to lift him up on to my saddle and to try to escape from the coffle. But my camel would not change direction. It was a fearful sensation. I felt that I was being carried inexorably towards some unknown but predetermined destination.

Towards sunset, in my dreams, I could see an Arab village of single-storeyed mud huts in the distance. Outside the village, the coffle was halted, and the slaves were closely hobbled together for the night. One of the traders, who carried a gun, was left behind to mount guard over them.

But I noticed that they did not hobble Awaad. Then the tallest trader—a lean, hook-nosed man, with his face pitted and scarred by smallpox—seized hold of Awaad's hand and dragged him towards the largest house in the village.

By then, my camel had knelt down and I had dismounted, and I now felt myself moving along beside them. But no villagers came out to greet us. The small main street was completely empty. I felt that I was entering a village of the dead.

Outside the main house, at the end of the street, the tall trader stopped in front of a brass-nail studded door and knocked five times in a curious rhythm. It was obviously a signal. A moment later, the door was opened by a servant dressed in a clean white turban and galabiah. The servant greeted the slaver and gave him a sly smile of complicity as he glanced down at little Awaad. I was not surprised that he did not notice me, because—by that time—I had realised that I was invisible to all of them.

The servant closed the door. We followed him into a small hall. On a table there was a leather money-pouch, tied about with a red silk cord. The servant gave the pouch to the trader, who nodded his head and left the house. The servant, about thirty years of age, smooth-faced and unpleasantly effeminate, leered at Awaad, put his hand round the boy's neck and led him to a door which opened off the hall.

Once again the servant struck the door five times. The door was opened a crack, and the servant pushed Awaad gently through it.

Immediately, I found I was in the room with the boy.

The lamp-lit room was furnished with plain village tables and benches. But the divan which ran the entire length of one side of the room was covered with expensively embroidered covers. The floor was strewn with rich carpets from Cairo.

At the end of the room stood Zubair, the famous slave-dealer.

Zubair looked at least ten years younger than when I had

met him recently in Cairo. He was naked except for a crimson sash around his waist. Zubair glanced at the young boy in silence. He crossed to the door and locked it. His dark skin was scarred by the wounds he had received in various battles. He was even more startlingly well-developed than my servant, Khalil. All his limbs seemed heavy with power. He took five paces towards the boy, and stood beside him examining him carefully. Soon he began stroking Awaad's cheek.

Meanwhile I was using every particle of my strength of will to free myself from the wooden bench on which I was sitting, but I could not move an inch. I sat horrified, forced to watch all that presently took place.

Frantically I tried to struggle from my bench. It was completely useless. I could not move. But my gaze was fixed compulsively on that ghastly spectacle of cruelty.

I awoke in my bed in Khartoum to the sound of desultory firing from the Dervish lines. Sweat was pouring off me and my bed was a tangled mass of damp sheets.

13 January

This morning I asked Khalil to find little Awaad duties in the kitchens of the Palace. After my disgusting dream, I could not bear to look at the boy. I was filled with a loathing of what the flesh can make of the spirit.

I have sent one of my spies to Major Kitchener, with the Expeditionary Force, telling him that Khartoum cannot hope to hold out for more than a fortnight at the very best. I have also given instructions that Zubair should not be allowed to come up to Khartoum to replace me as Governor-General, as I once suggested. I can now think of no more dangerous course than this.

I am sure that my evil, disgusting dream was meant as a warning to me.

The heat is sometimes as desperate as my own despair.

I look down on the herons and the malibou storks dipping at leisure into the muddy river, and I envy them. Then, in my stupid moments, I think were I a heron, I would fly away—at least for a while. But where could I fly to? Not to Cairo. Not even to London. For I now have enemies there as bitterly opposed to me as that false Messiah, the Mahdi, on the opposite bank. More bitter—because I have broken both the formal military *and* diplomatic rules. I am the outsider to their conventions. While I was successful they would put up with my little quirks and self-made decisions. If I fail, they will blame me, because my conduct did not conform to their book of rules. I shall be censured, and I have no doubt that a Court of Enquiry will follow. Such a Court I should enjoy. For it would give me the opportunity to tell the truth about the vacillations of the Ministers in London, of the hide-bound Generals in the War Office, and of that oily Ambassador, Baring, in Cairo, all of whom have, by their indecision and incompetence, caused the present condition of my poor Garrison in Khartoum.

If Khartoum is relieved, I shall go down as a hero. If Khartoum falls, I shall be presented to the public as a General who defied his orders—only because I tried to protect an innocent people from mutilation and murder, rather than obey such contradictory orders as I could decipher from the Establishment, and betray the many thousands who trusted in me.

In spite of the constant pounding of the Dervishes' guns we are able to continue with the work of reconstruction of the lines—necessitated by the receding of the Nile's waters. As the Nile recedes, the dangers of Khartoum become more apparent. Babylon was taken by the river Euphrates; and, through the rising of the Tigris, Nineveh fell. This is an odd coincidence. The Euphrates and the Tigris caused the fall of those two Empires. Now is it possible that the greatest of all the rivers of the ancient world will bring about the fall of another city? This city of Khartoum which I am defending is an outpost against the swirling, violent tide of Eastern fanaticism. If the Nile falls any further this year the Mahdi, and his followers, may be able to make their way, from the opposite bank, over the mudflats, and they may reach Khartoum.

The Dervishes fired four shells at the Palace at daybreak with no effect. Since then they have fired four more; one burst close to my room—a little high. I have put two guns near the Palace to reply to them. A report in town says that Waled a Goun's men are passing over from the right bank of the White Nile to the Mahdi's camp on the left bank. The Dervishes opened fire again on the Palace; and we answered their fire. They now have two guns firing on us. There is a report that the Mahdi's troops are going North (on the left bank of the White Nile).

We have silenced our friends opposite, having concentrated a heavy fire on them. I nearly lost my eyes this morning, firing on the Dervishes, when the base of the brass cartridge blew out, and sent the fire into my face; this is a fault of the Remington; the metal case of this cartridge must not be used too often.

Some people ought to have their heads cut off, if there is to be any quiet in the Sudan. I wonder how our Government will allow this to be done under their nose. For however necessary it may be to cut their heads off, if one is to assure the future peace of the Sudan, these people could scarcely be called rebels, because they could argue they were forced into rebellion by the inability of the Government aiding them. Also they could plead that they had heard the Sudan was to be abandoned.

Another battle! with the Dervishes at Goba, who, however, have no guns—firing terrific. Now the battle is over and we have won. The Dervishes are silent.

They began the battle again by firing their gun. When the battle was over, one of my own men was standing throwing dust in the air (like Shimei dusting David—'Thou bloody man'. 2 Samuel xvi 8). The Dervishes must have used up a lot of ammunition, for they kept up a steady fire, though where the bullets went no one could see. The Palace and the North Fort being high, our bullets reach *them*, but *their* bullets do not appear even to reach the river. They have a regular casement for the two guns, one directed on the Palace, and one on the North Fort. They took two days to make it, quite a creditable piece of work, with a screen wall in front. In the Crimea it was supposed and considered mean to bob, to avoid the enemy fire, and one used to try not to do so. A friend of mine used to say, 'It is all well enough for you, but I am a family man', and he used to bob at every report.

For my part I think judicious bobbing is not a fault, for I remember seeing, on two occasions, shells aiming straight towards me, which certainly, had I not bobbed, would have taken off my head. ('*And a good riddance too!*' The Foreign Office would have said.)

I make these remarks with reference to the Dervish rifle-fire; you can see them, with the telescope, aim directly at this wing of the Palace. You can see them fire, and then one hears a thud in the water. I have become quite accustomed to them by now. The milrailleuse (a Gatling) moved them out of their cover this evening; we have it on the Muduriat. The Palace roof is thus—

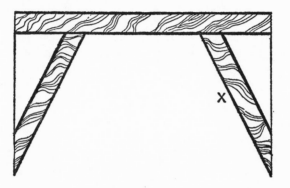

A shell striking at point X would bring down the roof, so when the Arabs fire, and one hears the sigh of the shell falling through the air, one does not feel comfortable until one hears it fall. The Palace is at least forty feet in height, but with only two storeys. The Pasha who built it, constructed it without leave from the old Khedive, taking funds to which he had no right. The old Khedive did not see it, but Ismail Pasha, then a prisoner here, split upon the builder. He was tried here, and, they say, was poisoned. Ismail Pasha took his place. Ismail Pasha was sent away because he did not treat one of the cast-off wives of the old Khedive, whom he was forced to marry, with proper respect; so this wife got up a harem intrigue, and poor Ismail Pasha was exiled.

Ismail Pasha was a great scamp, whatever was the cause of his exile. He belonged to Kurdistan, and was originally a bugler in Said Pasha's band. I used to tell him he was as much a foreigner in the land as I was.

A slave who came in says the Mahdi's return to Kordofan is cut off by an insurrection at his rear. So we are both like two rats in a box. (I wish *he* was *out* of the box!)

Truly, I am worn to a shadow with this food question; it is one continual demand. Five men deserted today.

I have a mystical feeling that I am destined to meet the Mahdi face to face some day. Should we ever meet, in a calm and sober stmosphere, free from the bitterness of this civil war, there is even the possibility that we may find much to discuss of common interest.

16 January

I have never been afraid of Death, only of the pains of my body and the anguish of my spirit, and the misery of my temptations.

If only I could write in honesty that smoking too many cigarettes every day and that drinking too much brandy were my only temptations, I could face life with equanimity.

As a child, as soon as I was old enough to become conscious of the desires of my flesh, I knew that my body could drag me down into iniquity.

When I was fourteen, I was made so wretched by my temptations that I wrote a letter to the clergyman who was preparing me for confirmation, in which I confessed that each night I prayed to God *to make me a eunuch* in order that I might avoid the temptations of my flesh . . .

When I went to the Crimea, I must admit that I hoped to be killed—without having a hand in it myself. But I survived and lived. At that stage I did not wish to become too closely acquainted with God, nor yet did I wish to leave Him. My religious views were valuable to me because—like a great-coat—they protected me from the lusts of my flesh. But with each year that I lived, God grew closer to me, until now at this present day I feel that He is responsible for all my thoughts and for all my actions. Yet my desires have not decreased. On the contrary. I am afraid that they are as keen as ever.

But I know for certain that all that the flesh admires is doomed. Cursed is the man who makes flesh his aim.

For this reason I have never given in to the commands of my fleshly desires. From my youth I have prayed for a complete deliverance from my particular temptations . . .

My prayers saved me both in China and in the Congo. I loved the boys I tried to help. However difficult the launching of a new campaign might be, however hard the fighting was, however arduous my work—I found time to help lost or orphaned boys. I took them under my care. I fed them. I made friends with them. I tried to find employment for them. I loved them. But no sin entered into my relationship with them.

I keep the brandy decanter on the far side of my Operations Room so that, at night, I have quite a walk from the desk in my bedroom to reach it. But I must confess that a few minutes ago—after a hopeless look through my telescope—I went to the table at the far end of the Operations Room and drank heavily. A man must be wretched if he can live neither in the present, nor in the past, nor in the future.

I am forcing myself to live in the past—because I feel that if I learn to appreciate my past faults and weaknesses, then I may perhaps gain redemption before I die.

So tonight I will force my mind to dwell on some of the relationships I have had with these boys.

When I was training at Woolwich, I formed only casual friendships. I felt a constant yearning to find a close friend whom I could feel would belong to me—just as I would belong to him. But I was too shy to find such a person. And this frustration may well have led to the frantic outbursts of wildness and temper from which I suffered.

When I was sailing as a young Lieutenant to Constantinople, after the Crimean War, I found for myself a good-looking boy called Ivan whom I took on as my servant. Ivan was about eighteen years old, with black hair brushed sleekly back from his forehead. He had large dark eyes and a skin of alabaster. He was, I think, devoted to me. He was religious. He had only one fault. He could not be prevented from staring lasciviously at every young girl he saw. There was one servant girl in the employ of an elderly female passenger. Ivan seemed eager to form some close relationship with the girl. I was furiously jealous. I happened to meet the girl on deck. I spoke to her coldly. 'I do not intend to allow any relationship between you and Ivan,' I told her, 'because he belongs to me.'

This was mean and petty on my part. I realised it even at the time; and I was not surprised when Ivan left me in Constantinople.

In 1860, on the voyage out to Shanghai, I noticed a young steward whose face immediately attracted me. I found out that his name was Kirkham. He had a head of thickly growing red hair and remarkably green eyes. He was also gifted with a shy smile which he would bestow on me when he thought that no one else was looking.

A rather pompous English merchant who was travelling out to China—obviously in the hope of making a quick fortune—accused young Kirkham, the steward, of stealing money from him. As soon as I heard this I asked for Kirkham to be sent to my cabin. There I questioned him closely, and so sternly that after a while the poor boy broke down and cried. But he still refused to admit theft. By now,

I was convinced of his honesty. The sight of his smooth face, wet with tears, affected me strongly. Then and there I made my decision. I paid back an equal amount of money to the tiresome passenger who had complained that his cash had been stolen, and I took on Kirkham as my personal steward.

A few days before we reached Shanghai, however, I realised that there might have been some truth in the accusation against the young man. For small objects of little value began to disappear from my cabin. I had no proof that Kirkham was the culprit, but my suspicions were so strong that I made an excuse to get rid of him when we landed in Shanghai.

When I reached China and eventually took over the so-called Ever-Victorious Army, I had at least half a dozen Chinese boys in my retinue. I admired their delicacy. My Wangs, I called them—my little princes. Then, when I returned to England—to the acclamation of the Press and was called 'Chinese Gordon'—I was relegated to the position of Commander of the Gravesend defences so as to get me out of the way of the powers-that-be who were jealous of me.

The flesh as a substance is as useless as is the dust to which it must return. The flesh worships idols of silver and of gold. Its praise is the praise of men; its fears are for what men may say of it. As the Crucifixion was a slow death, so is our death a slow process of extermination for the flesh and its transitory ambitions. It makes us yearn for complete deliverance.

At the moment I can obtain a momentary oblivion only by finishing the brandy in the decanter.

When I returned to England from China, the Government, from fear or jealousy of me—or perhaps both—deliberately put me on the shelf. They made me Commander of the Royal Engineers at Gravesend, as I've said, with orders to direct the construction of some new forts for the defence of the Thames estuary.

I found the job footling.

'The world,' I wrote to Augusta at that time, 'is a vast prison house under hard keepers with hard rules. We are in cells—solitary and lonely, looking for relief.' I was in the dumps.

Gradually, however, I realised that in Gravesend there were important occupations demanding my most urgent attention.

First, I was outraged by the hypocrisy of the Established Church and of its members. I began to preach in any hall or chapel that would allow me to, and I began to write tracts.

'Explain oh preachers how it is that we ask and do not get comfort, that your cold services cheer not,' I wrote in one of my tracts of that period. 'You preach death as an enemy instead of a friend and liberator. Be as uncharitable as you like, you say, but attend my church regularly. Does your vast system of ceremonies, meetings and services tend to lessen sin in the world? It may make men conceal it. Where would you find more hardness to a fallen one than you would in a congregation of worshippers in the church of this day? Surely this hardness is of the devil and those who show it know not God ... Oh Pharisees of this day, ye ten-fold more self-righteous than the Pharisees of old ... Happy is it that there is a shepherd who does know and care for His sheep, for we would be in poor case if we fell in your hands. Fall down, oh ye mighty of the earth, ye Kings and warriors and priests and hide yourself from the face of Him who comes with all His people. He was hungry and thirsty and ye passed Him by. Little did you, in the days of your pride, think you turned the Royal Race from your doors and, by treading them down, trod down the King of Kings. Inasmuch as ye despised them, ye despised Him.

Leprosy is leprosy, whether it be covered by garments of silk or by rags. The self-righteous preachers and religious authorities of the outward church do all their works to be seen of men. They preach great sanctity and love and do not practise it themselves.'

Secondly, I discovered a task which was to absorb my energies during those long years I spent in Gravesend.

The small Fort House in which I lived lay in one of the poorest districts of England. I could not walk along the street without seeing some half-starved urchin. In the slums working on the barley boats and lighters, and in the cement works, there were boys who had been bullied and mal-treated almost from the day they had been born. Most of them were now homeless.

I decided to convert Fort House into a kind of lodging house for them. Each evening—after my work was over—I would walk out into the streets or down to the docks. Each evening, I would find some wretched boy, clothed in tatters, whose features would make me believe that he was worth helping. I would take the boy back to Fort House. I would undress him. I would bathe him. Indeed I would wash his slender little body with my own hands. Then I would lead the boy up to a room in which I had installed a large wardrobe. In it were suits of rough serge and woollen shirts, to fit almost any size of boy. I would clothe the boy. Then I would lead him to the long mirror in my bedroom and make him stand in front of it.

'Just as you see a new boy without,' I would tell him, 'so I want to see a new boy within.'

Later I would find him a job, or I would persuade him to enlist in the services.

Soon Fort House was almost full with these boys I had adopted. But even so, my desire to find new boys in order to help them did not abate. I began to search for them almost constantly. I was aware that some people in the neighbour-hood were suspicious of my intentions towards the boys. I did not care a rap. For at that period of my life it was only my love for these dirty, ragged boys that gave me the strength to continue living. To me, these boys running about the town all around me were worth millions—and I made no secret of that fact. I called them my Kings, my Wangs, my Doves, my Angels, my Scuttlers. In another letter which I wrote I can remember describing them as my 'lumps of flesh, red and white'.

Each of them attracted me in a different way. One might have an adorable little lisp. Another might be an ardent Hebrew lad of fourteen. A third might have a mischievous pug-face and still bear the traces of his father's belt on his back.

When a boy would leave Fort House to go out into the world I would ask him to write to me each week so that I could mark his whereabouts with a small individual flag on a map which I had hung behind my desk.

Even when I returned from Palestine and met Harry Scott with his catapult, I could not resist the impudent charm of the young ruffian, and I installed him that very day in our house in Rockstone Place. He stayed there for a few weeks after I'd left, so Augusta wrote to me. Then she persuaded him to enlist under the Colours.

More recently there has been little Awaad who escaped into our lines. Until I took Awaad on as a Palace servant, I had almost thought I had purged myself of my desires. But Awaad—together with my vile dream—has made me realise that I am still in the bondage of my despicable temptations.

I loved the boys I adopted—I loved them all . . . But I resisted temptation . . . You, God, know it. I did nothing wrong . . . But in my heart I wanted them. I desired them— and that, God, I know, was sin enough.

I have paused to light a cigarette. My hands are trembling.

I feel an apprehension as if some immediate struggle lay ahead of me.

Deliver me—deliver me, oh God, from my soiled body with its contemptible infirmities and horrible desires. Release me. Let me die . . .

In a kind of daze I have just read back through the last few pages of this journal. The effect of what I've read has been to send me to fetch brandy from the room next door and drink.

I am horrified by the implications of what I have written.

Can this be what it has all been about? Did I come out here to Khartoum only because I was yearning for death, but was afraid of accepting my nature and because I was afraid of committing the crime before God of killing myself?

Did I come out here to the Sudan in order to be killed?

If that is true, then a ghastly implication follows directly and inevitably from it. If I have stayed on in Khartoum because deep in my heart I yearn for death, then my private anguish has had the most appalling public consequences.

But can it be possible?

Can it be possible that the greatest Relief Expedition that England has ever mounted has been sent out here because one unimportant little man in this distant town wants to be killed in order to escape from his temptations?

Have hundreds of officers and thousands of men been sent out to Egypt and beyond, to suffer the miseries of warfare in the desert, and the callousness of this country—merely because of my personal wish to kill myself?

'No,' I cry to myself. 'No . . . it's inconceivable, and I refuse—drunk or sober—to believe it.'

These pages have recorded the thoughts of a dispirited and weary man. The real truth is that I came out here to save the Sudan from massacre or slavery. And here I will stay until the Relief Expedition comes.

Today, when I was up on the Palace roof, searching the horizon for any signs of the Relief Force, I observed disturbances in the Mahdi's camp. Great crowds of the Dervish women were weeping and wailing. The Mahdi's forces had just fired a victory salute of one hundred and one guns. But I knew intuitively that this salute must be some kind of blind. Obviously the Dervishes have suffered a defeat at the hands of the advancing forces of the Relief Expedition.

Though I have been pretty well dispirited for the last few days, a part of me cannot help laughing at the fearful mess we are in. I am here to help the people of the Sudan, but the Relief Expedition seems to have come out here only to save me. If this is the case I shall stay put and do what I can with what military supplies they will leave for me.

Late tonight, as if to confirm my resolution to stay, one of my spies managed to get through the Mahdi's lines and enter Khartoum with magnificent news.

The British Expeditionary Force has gained a great victory over the Mahdi's Dervishes at Abu Klea. I know this country so well that I can work out the movements of the Expeditionary Force. They should reach the Metemma by 22 January and, at the latest, should be in Khartoum by 25 January. The news has spread like wildfire through the town. There has been much public rejoicing.

This victory explains, then, the lamenting Dervish women I observed this morning. They were the widows of the fallen.

I feel almost faint with joy. I have been justified. I made the right decision when I decided to hold out against the Mahdi. I may well—yet—be called the Saviour of the Sudan.

When I was shaving myself this morning, I was intent, as usual, on the mere manipulations of my razor. Suddenly my attention was arrested by the full sight of my face in the mirror. I found myself staring at the face of a stranger.

I saw a haggard man, well past middle-age, with his hair snowy-white, his face ravaged with lines of anxiety and fatigue. The eyes must once have been bright, but the eyes watching me from the mirror had no lustre in them, only a dullness caused by worry and despair.

Throughout the day odd thoughts have come creeping into my mind. I am so utterly weary of the Sudanese, with whom I have to deal continually, that I find that I am now often tempted to abandon them and to escape down the Nile. I declare solemnly that, if it were not for the honour's sake of my nation, I would let these people slide. They are of the feeblest nature. The Arabs are ten times better. But because these people are weak, there is so much more reason to try and help them. I think it was because we are such worthless creatures that Our Lord came to deliver us.

Also, all day, I have been aware of thousands of cranes flying over Khartoum. They have a curious cry which reminds me, in some fanciful way, of the poems of Schiller, which few people read, but which I admire greatly. (Though I know them only in translation.)

The sniping today has been far more frequent. The Dervishes have begun to shell the Palace regularly, from across the Nile.

Towards sunset, when I walked into my Operations Room, I found my Commander-in-Chief, Faregh, alone in the room. He was staring despondently through the French windows.

'I wanted to see you, ya sidi,' he replied. At that instant I sensed that he was expecting an almost immediate invasion of the town.

'There's a great deal of movement in the enemy's lines,' I said crisply. 'They may attack towards dawn. But the Relief Force will arrive at any moment now. In the meantime, go back to your post.'

I walked out on to the balcony and went to the telescope. I looked through it. The telescope is now always pointing in the same direction—down the Nile, in the hope that through it I may detect the smoke of the steamers, some sign of the Expeditionary Force.

Faregh followed me and stood by the window.

'I must talk to your Excellency,' he said.

Grimly I turned away from the telescope and walked back into the room.

'What is it, Faregh?' I asked.

For a moment he was silent. I could see that he was hesitating over which words he should use.

'The Mahdi has sent me a letter,' he announced after a pause.

'What does the Mahdi say?' I asked.

Faregh spoke slowly and deliberately. Sweat glistened on his stolid black face.

' "The British Expedition has been defeated," the Mahdi says,' Faregh announced to me. 'He offers us honourable terms if we surrender the Garrison. Otherwise he will break into Khartoum and kill every man in it.'

'Do you believe such lies?' I asked. 'Do you believe that the British forces have been defeated by a horde of Dervishes? You know that only nine days ago the British had a victory at Abu Klea, less than fifty miles from the Nile. Through your glasses with your own eyes you have seen the Dervish women mourning for their thousand dead. You know the Mahdi must have suffered a defeat.'

'We also know that Fort Omdurman has fallen,' Faregh replied obstinately. 'We know that the Nile is sinking lower

We know too that the *Abbas* was captured and that the Englishmen were killed. We know, also, that there is no hope for us.'

'Do you honestly believe that the Mahdi would spare the people of Khartoum?' I asked him. 'The Mahdi hasn't forgotten that a month ago I opened the town gates to let out all who would join him. From that he knows that all who remain must be against him.'

The lines of Faregh's heavy face were set in a defiant obstinacy.

'For more than four months you tell the people that a British force is on its way,' he said. 'But no British troops appear. My men are sick. They can hardly stand. There is no food for them. They have eaten even dogs and rats and the juice of the date trees. They are sick and weak. And their hearts are sick. The Garrison can hold out no more. We are finished.'

I girded myself to one last effort.

'I tell you on my word of honour, I am certain that the British will arrive, if not tomorrow, then certainly within the next two days,' I said. 'This is the last appeal I shall ever make to you. You have resisted the Mahdi's forces for very nearly a year. I now ask you to resist for only another forty-eight hours.'

'It may not be possible,' Faregh said.

At once I guessed the reason.

'Have you shown the Mahdi's letter to the town notables?' I asked him sharply.

Faregh nodded his over-large head.

'You should not have done so without consulting me,' I told him.

I turned and walked out on to the verandah. I had to control the rage I could feel beginning to rise within me. I went to the telescope. The light was going by now. A cool night breeze was blowing.

Faregh followed me out and stood by my side.

'I beg your Excellency's pardon,' Faregh said in an expressionless voice.

I moved the telescope slightly. 'Look!' I cried. 'Isn't that a steamer's smoke on the horizon?'

I moved from the eyepiece of the glass, and Faregh peered through it.

'No,' he replied, looking up, 'it is only the smoke from the enemy cannons.'

He turned to go. A grim thought suddenly came to me.

'Faregh,' I said, 'your officer in charge of the section of our lines where the Nile is most shallow is surely Omar Ibrahim? I haven't seen him all day. Is he sick?'

Faregh hesitated.

'Perhaps he is sick,' he answered after a pause.

'He's one of your officers,' I said. 'You must know if he's ill or not.'

Faregh swallowed. Then he turned his face away from me so that I could not see his eyes.

'Omar Ibrahim has left,' he said slowly. 'He has gone over to the Mahdi.'

I felt the rage seething all through me like some awful burning pain. My control snapped completely.

'And Omar was the very officer you wanted to promote,' I shouted at Faregh. 'Can't you even judge the officers under you? Don't you realise that he will have taken the plans of our defences with him?'

Faregh made no reply. But he shifted his feet uncomfortably and gazed at me sullenly.

'Answer me!' I shouted at him.

'A month ago you let many people go over to the Mahdi,' Faregh answered, almost insolently.

'But they were civilians,' I said. 'And you know perfectly well that civilians are never allowed anywhere near our defence works.'

'Other officers would like to do as Omar,' Faregh said in

a tone of voice which sounded as if he felt he had scored an important debating point.

I was very close to unleashing the full fury of my rage. But, somehow, I still controlled myself.

'They would go over to the Mahdi because they have lost heart,' I explained. 'But it's our business to encourage them. In every section of the line I visited tonight I talked to the officers and men. I tried to give them hope. You must do the same.'

'It is not possible,' Faregh stated. 'We must surrender.'

His obstinate attitude of defeatism finally broke the cords which held back the full violence of my fury.

'You idiot,' I cried. 'We shall never surrender.'

'You cannot stop us,' Faregh answered. He had now become openly defiant.

I strode towards him and slapped him hard across the face. For a moment I thought he would set on me. Though he is a powerfully-built man I would have welcomed it. Then I could have tried to strike him down. My anger would have lent me strength. But he did not move. He just glared at me in sullen animosity.

'Just remember this,' I said to him. 'If the Dervishes break through our defence lines at any point, Khartoum is lost Once they have broken through our defences, there is nothing we can do—except wait to be murdered.'

Faregh kept silent. I decided that our confrontation had lasted long enough.

I dismissed him curtly.

'Now get back to your post,' I said. 'The White Nile end of the lines is our weakest point now that the river's so low. See to it that they're alert there.'

For an instant an ugly look of temper showed in Faregh's face. Then he saluted smartly and left the room.

As if drawn by a magnet, I went back to the telescope on the verandah. After another look I left it, and walked wearily back into my bedroom. I noticed the Bible lying open on my desk.

I turned to my favourite Psalm. I will make myself write down these words which comfort me the most—because even as I read the words I can feel some measure of peace flowing into my troubled heart. These words drive the bitterness and fury of my temper from me. They are like a soothing balm.

These are the words:

'Yea, though I walk through the valley of the shadow of death, I will fear no evil; for Thou art with me; Thy rod and Thy staff they comfort me. Surely goodness and mercy shall follow me all the days of my life. And I shall dwell in the house of the Lord for ever.'

I have been staring out at the night. The moon is sinking closer to the horizon, and it is growing darker. The Dervishes are silent now, and the stillness is only broken by the occasional howling of a surviving dog, and the small noises of the night creatures.

I have beside me a tin of cigarettes, and some brandy. It is impossible to sleep, and these will help me reach the dawn.

24 January

There is no news from the Expeditionary Force. We should have heard something from them by now. The fleeting moment of excitement over the victory at Abu Klea has turned into despondency and despair. The Mahdi has sent messengers into the town to spread the word amongst the populace that I have lied. These messengers have said that I invented the victory at Abu Klea to boost the morale of the town and harden them in their resistance to the Mahdi. These false messengers have even claimed that in truth it was the British who were defeated at Abu Klea, and that it was a great triumph for the Dervishes.

I continue to urge the notables and townspeople to make one final effort to hold Khartoum. But they are exhausted and starving. Many still die daily. They have little strength left. Because the British redcoats do not appear they begin to believe that I have lied.

There is only one other European in Khartoum, Martin Hansall, the Austrian Consul. But I will have nothing to do with him. He stayed behind only to be with his seven female attendants, and I have heard that he is disposed to go over with these females to the Dervishes. I hope that he will do so. Otherwise I am quite alone.

Through my telescope I can see the Mahdi massing his forces. The hordes of Dervishes bow down before him. The noise from their strange musical instruments drifts on the breeze across the river to us. Their flags of red and black and green are raised up. It is only a matter of time now before the final assault comes. And I fear that Khartoum is too weak now to hold out.

Omar Ibrahim knew that the White Nile was very low at some points. He knew where the water was shallow and the mudflats made it easy to cross. Now that he has gone over to the Mahdi, he is sure to have handed on this information.

The Mahdi has started to move his troops across the Nile to the right bank. Looking at the people who surround me, I see only ill-concealed signs of treachery and hatred. I calculate that a mass of the populace of Khartoum would now be willing to become subjects of the Mahdi. These Sudanese are not worth any great sacrifice. Yet I have an admiration for my enemies. The very meanest of the Mahdi's followers is a determined warrior, who can undergo any privation, and who no more cares about pain or death than if he were a stone.

The scales are heavily balanced against me. Again and again I scan the horizon for some sign of the Relief Expedition, but I see none. It is, of course, on the cards that Khartoum will be taken under the very nose of the Expeditionary Force, which will arrive *just too late*.

The beautiful, proud hawks that wheel and cry about the Palace remind me of a passage in the Bible. I transcribe the words here:

> 'The eye that mocketh at his father and despiseth to obey his mother, the ravens of the valley shall pick it out, and the young eagles shall eat it.'

It can be no child's play to be captured by the Mahdi. I often wonder, as I watch those hawks, if they are destined to pick out my eyes.

25 January, 2 a.m.

I am writing these words sitting at the large mahogany desk in my Operations Room. I have various reasons for writing at this time of night. The main one is to distract me from my bedroom next door.

I am fully aware that this may be my last entry in this journal. I am uncertain whether these next twenty-four hours will end in victory or in defeat.

Last night I had finished the entry in this journal for 24 January at about eleven p.m. Then, as usual, I made my tour of the defences. An hour later, I came back to the Operations Room and helped myself to a brandy and soda. Presently my servant Khalil came in and told me that the merchant Bordeini was waiting downstairs to see me. I told Khalil to show him up.

Bordeini came in looking tired and said. He had once been a very fat man, but now his clothes seemed to hang loosely on him. As he approached me I saw that he was close to tears. In a pathetic way, he tried to smile as he began his usual gambit.

'The blessing of Allah be upon you, General Gordon.' he said.

I tried to smile back at him.

'And on you, Bordeini Bey,' I answered—according to our book of rules.

'I trust your Excellency is in good health,' Bordeini continued.

'Thanks be to God,' I began. Then I broke off because suddenly there was a gulp in my throat.

'Oh, Bordeini, I've no heart for our usual fencing.' I said. 'What brings you to see me at this late hour?'

Bordeini's hands began to flutter and tug at his clothes.

'The town notables have been meeting,' he answered. 'They have been discussing the letter that the Mahdi writes to Faregh Pasha.'

I gestured towards the bottle of brandy on the drinks-tray. Bordeini bowed his head in thanks and crossed to the table.

'What have the notables decided?' I asked.

Bordeini splashed a little soda on top of the brandy in his glass and took a long drink.

'They wish to surrender tonight,' he said in a voice of complete despair. 'They believe it is their last chance of life.'

I held out my tin of cigarettes towards Bordeini. He bowed again and this time shook his head. As I lit my cigarette, a silly thought slid into my mind. I reflected that at least the departure of the Europeans had preserved the supplies of liquor and tobacco.

'The steamers carrying the British troops may arrive at any moment now,' I said to Bordeini.

Bordeini nodded and looked up at me—like a child who has been lied to by a parent whom he loves.

'I tell them so,' he said. 'I tell them, "Tonight the steamers will arrive. Gordon Pasha has said so." But they will not believe me. They say: "No. We listened to the Pasha for almost a full year of siege. But now at last we know that he has deceived us." '

I helped myself to another drink.

'How can they doubt a British Force is coming?' I asked. 'They have seen the very letter announcing the fact—the letter signed by the Expedition's Intelligence Officer, Major Kitchener.

Bordeini sighed. 'They do not believe the letter,' he stated.

'Do they think I forged it?' I asked.

Bordeini hesitated. I noticed, for the first time, how slackly the folds of flesh now hung about his face.

'Perhaps,' he answered.

Outside it was very quiet. The sniping and shelling had temporarily ceased. The night was cooling, and the sky was very clear.

'Do *you* believe I forged it?' I asked him.

Bordeini shook his head vigorously.

'No, Excellency,' he answered. 'But they do not listen to me.'

I looked into Bordeini's large, dark eyes. I forced conviction into my voice.

'I am certain that the steamers will arrive before dawn.' I said. 'I know it instinctively. I feel it in my bones. I feel they're getting nearer.'

As I spoke, a sudden instinct told me that the Expeditionary Force was even at that instant approaching Khartoum.

'Bordeini,' I said quietly, 'go out on to the verandah and look through the telescope. You will see on the horizon the smoke of the steamers at last. I'm sure of it.'

Bordeini went out on to the verandah and went to the telescope. I could see him peering through the lens. I remained motionless in the room. My fists were clenched at my sides. I was praying more intensely than I have ever prayed in my life.

For a while there was silence. Then I saw Bordeini lift his head from the telescope. Slowly he walked back into the room.

'There is nothing, Excellency,' he said, almost in a whisper.

'But they will come,' I said. 'I know they will.'

Bordeini said nothing. But once again his hands were moving uneasily. He was a dishonest man, yet between us there had sprung up some kind of mutual respect.

'I've got enough food for only one more day,' I said. 'Haven't you got a few ardebs of doura hidden away?'

I am convinced that Bordeini answered me with complete sincerity.

'No,' he replied. 'Even I go hungry this last week.'

Bordeini took a gulp of his drink.

'Excellency, what must I say to the Council?' he asked. 'They are waiting for me to return with an answer from you.'

'Tell them that I promise that the British troops will be in Khartoum before dawn,' I said. 'Tell them that they have held out for nearly a year—and now I ask them to hold out for a few more hours. If the steamers aren't here by dawn and they prefer to submit, I will give Faregh Pasha orders to open the gates and let every single inhabitant of this town join the rebels.'

Bordeini bowed his head sadly.

'I will tell them your words, Excellency,' he mumbled.

'What more can I say?' I asked wearily. 'I have told them over and over again that help would be here, but it's never come. How can they be blamed for not believing me? If this, my last promise, fails, I can do nothing more.'

'There is still one of your ships left,' Bordeini said. 'It has steam up. You could still get away.'

Suddenly my mind switched away from the lamp-lit room in the Palace at Khartoum, and I saw Augusta—as stern-looking as ever—standing in the drawing-room at Rock-stone Place. I could see her very clearly; I could see her grey hair and the firm lines around her mouth. She stood slim and very straight, and I felt that she was looking at me.

Then I noticed that behind her was a map of the Sudan. I gazed almost involuntarily, at the map with its clear demarcations of Khartoum and the valley of the Nile. But as I gazed, suddenly the black lines of the river began to stir and then to writhe, and I saw that at the point where the Nile should have joined the sea there was the long head of a snake.

I shut my eyes. For an instant I was afraid that I was going mad. When I opened my eyes again, Bordeini was watching me anxiously. I struggled to fix my attention on Bordeini's last words. I tried to make myself realise the import of what he had said. I was in a prison, but I could still escape. I could get away from Khartoum with its flies and stench and dust and heat. If my last little steamer was not holed by the Mahdi's fire, I might reach safety; I might even reach Cairo.

I could leave this withered and tormented Continent, and retire to the peace of England, with its trim villages and well-watered fields. But then—with a lurch of sadness—I remembered the promises I had made.

'No,' I said. 'After all the support I've had from the people here, it would be the climax of meanness to desert them. I *must* stay. But you can go, Bordeini.'

'No,' Bordeini answered. 'I am staying.'

'And if the town falls?' I asked.

Bordeini glanced out towards the river, then stared down at his large plump hands.

'You must not worry for me,' he said.

'You can get out?' I asked him.

Immediately I noticed that Bordeini looked embarrassed.

'They will not kill me,' Bordeini said. 'I have too much money hidden outside Khartoum . . . And the Mahdi has a daughter, very young, very nice.'

I managed to smile.

'Oh, Bordeini,' I said. 'You would become a Dervish and wear those filthy clothes?'

Bordeini's mouth twitched.

'Only until I had married a Dervish,' he answered.

I smiled once more.

'You're a rogue, Bordeini,' I said. 'But I'm glad you're my friend—for now you must help me. Go to the Council. Tell them my words. Do your best to persuade them.'

Bordeini moved towards the door.

'I will,' he said. 'May Allah preserve us all this night.'

As Bordeini spoke, Khalil came in. He was carrying an envelope. Immediately I saw that it was grimy and encrusted with seals. Khalil handed me the envelope. As soon as I looked at the outside of the envelope I recognised the handwriting.

'This is Kitchener's writing,' I cried out to Bordeini. 'Wait.'

My fingers were trembling so much that I could hardly open the letter, and when I had unfolded it, my excitement was so intense that I could scarcely read it.

This letter from Kitchener was dated three days previously, on 22 January. In it, Kitchener announced—with his usual precision and clarity—the magnificent news that the British forces had captured Metemma and joined up with my steamers. The troops were embarking. The Commander, Colonel Sir Charles Wilson, expected that the steamers would reach Khartoum before 3 a.m. on 26 January. Khartoum would be relieved before dawn that day.

I was near to tears. I did not trust my voice. I handed the letter to Bordeini in silence. As he read it through I could see his flabby jowls quivering with emotion. He raised the letter to his lips and kissed it.

'Your promise has been kept,' he said. 'Now for always they will believe you, Excellency.'

He stretched out his hand to give the letter to me. But I shook my head.

'You must keep the letter,' I told him.

I began to pace up and down. I was so feverish that I had to keep moving.

'First send the news to Faregh,' I told Bordeini. 'Then show your Council the letter. Let every man, woman and child in the town be told that Khartoum will be relieved before dawn the day after tomorrow. Go quickly and then come back to me.'

Bordeini moved towards the door. Then he turned.

'I need not now ask Allah's blessing for you,' he said, 'for he has blessed you already.'

Then he went out.

I turned to Khalil who was watching me, and grinning joyfully.

'Who brought this message?' I asked.

'One of your people, ya sidi,' he answered.

At first I could not understand.

'One of my people?' I asked in amazement.

'When he comes to the gate, he is wearing the djelleba of a Dervish,' Khalil explained, 'and mud covers his face. But when he comes inside, he wipes the mud away and his skin is white.'

'Where is he?' I asked.

'Waiting downstairs, ya sidi,' Khalil replied.

'Ask him to come up,' I said.

Khalil bowed and went out. As soon as he had left the room I knelt down to thank God for deliverance. Then I walked quickly to the windows and looked out into the darkness. But I could see no lights on the river. I came back into the room and lit a cigarette.

Presently the main door opened and a young man walked in and stood rigidly to attention, at the entrance to the room. His khaki shirt and slacks were covered with mud which was beginning to dry. His wet curly hair was plastered down on his forehead. His face was still streaked with mud. But there was something familiar about the broad mouth and wide-set eyes, and the features of his face.

He gazed towards me enquiringly. He was obviously nervous, yet, in some way, he seemed expectant.

I looked at him wonderingly. 'Come in,' I said.

The young man took a few uncertain steps into the room. Khalil closed the main door behind him, and went off.

I could now see that the young man was only a boy. Perhaps he was seventeen. There was something very attractive about him.

'How did you get through the Dervish lines?' I asked him.

'Waited till it was dark,' the boy answered in a gentle Cockney accent. 'Then crept up the Nile. Tried to swim a bit but the current was too strong.'

Suddenly, as I stared at him, I recognised the boy.

'But you're Harry,' I said. 'You're Harry Scott who broke up my sister's Mission School in Southampton.'

The boy's head jerked back as if I had struck him.

'No, sir,' he cried out. It was a cry of protest. Suddenly he looked sullen, almost hostile.

'But you did,' I said. 'I remember it perfectly well. You used a catapult. And then you stayed in our house in Rockstone Place until you joined the Army.'

'No, sir,' the boy answered. 'I'm Willie Warren. Trooper Warren, now, sir.'

For an instant the name meant nothing to me.

'Don't you remember, sir?' the boy asked. 'It's less than three years ago. I was hanging around the docks. I hadn't had a decent meal for weeks . . .'

At that moment, it came back to me.

'Wait,' I interrupted. 'I *can* remember. My memory may

have gone all to pieces, but I remember you very well. You are indeed Willie Warren. You'd run away from your home in London because you and some of your friends had broken into a pawnbroker's shop. You thought that the police were after you. I remember that I found you one evening on the docks at Southampton lying against a derelict winch. I took you back to our house in Rockstone Place.'

As I spoke his face brightened.

'So you haven't forgotten, sir,' the boy said.

'Of course I haven't,' I answered. 'I took you back and gave you a good bath and a large supper. You stayed in our house even after I'd left for Palestine. Then, my sister told me in one of her letters, you joined the Colours.'

Suddenly Willie swayed and only just managed to stop himself from falling.

I pointed to a chair. 'Sit down,' I said.

I went quickly to the drinks-table and poured out a little brandy. When I came back with it, Willie tried to get up.

'Sit down,' I said. 'And that's an order.'

Willie took a gulp of brandy and choked a little. Then he took a small sip and licked his lips.

'It's got our grog fair beat,' he said.

'Feeling better now?' I asked.

I observed the strange contrast, now, of his curly dark-brown, nearly black, hair and his light violet eyes.

'Yes, thank you, sir,' the boy answered.

'You must be hungry,' I said. 'Shall I ask Khalil to bring you some food?'

'No thanks, sir,' Willie answered. 'I couldn't eat just now. But I'll be all right later.'

He was now far more at ease. The strained expression had left his face.

'You left Metemma three days ago?' I asked him.

'Yes, sir,' he replied.

'How many steamers were there at Metemma?' I enquired.

'Three, sir.'

'All serviceable?'

'Having trouble with one of them,' Willie said. 'But the other two were fine, sir. They were leaving right away.'

'Can you remember their names?' I asked.

'The big one was called the *Bordein*,' Willie replied.

'That's correct. The other will have been the *Talahawein*,' I said. 'How many troops are there at Metemma?'

'Nearly a thousand, sir.'

'A hundred could save us,' I said. 'Have you had many casualties?'

'About three hundred,' Willie answered. 'Sir Herbert Stewart and Colonel Burnaby were killed near Metemma. Colonel Wilson's in command now, sir.'

'How many troops are they sending on the steamers?' I asked.

'I don't know, sir,' Willie replied. 'But I do know that Colonel Wilson's got red coats for the men to wear.'

'Then it doesn't matter how few they are,' I said. 'Once the people of Khartoum see the red coats, the trick will be done. They'll know the British are here. That's all we need.'

Willie grinned.

'The British will be here all right,' he said. 'And there's more coming up behind. You should of seen us the first day we left for Metemma on our camels. Laugh! I nearly fell off it meself.'

I went over to him.

'Willie, I'm glad that you came tonight,' I said. 'Do you know that yours is the first white face I've seen in over four months? And yours isn't very white.'

Willie took my attempt at a joke with extreme seriousness.

'I'll have a wash before I turn in, sir,' he answered.

I could not bear the thought of the boy leaving me at this point, but I realised how tired he must be from his long journey. I felt obliged to give him the opportunity of going to bed.

'You must be tired. Would you like to turn in now?' I asked him.

Willie stared at me with his violet eyes.

'When I've been waiting for this moment for the last three months?' he replied. 'Not likely! Unless I'm in the way, sir.'

'No, Willie,' I said—and I was shocked to discover there was a tremor in my voice. 'You're not in the way.'

'Do you always stay up all night, sir?' he asked.

'They tell me I'm a fool,' I replied, 'because there's nothing to do until dawn after I've been round the defences at two or three in the morning. But if I go to bed I can't sleep, or I have the most ghastly nightmares. Besides, I'm certain that it will be at night that the Dervishes will try to break through. I get my sleep during the day when I'm lucky.'

I handed Willie a cigarette.

'I bet you're looking forward to seeing the lights of London again, sir,' Willie said.

'I want to see my sister again. But not London,' I answered. 'I shall go straight back to work in the Congo. I tell you, Willie, I dwell on the joy of never seeing London again, with its horrid wearisome dinner-parties and miseries. How people put up with it passes my imagination. It's a perfect bondage. We're all in masks, saying what we don't believe, eating and drinking things we don't want, and then abusing one another. I'd sooner live like a Dervish with the Mahdi than go out to dinner every night in London. If any English General comes to Khartoum I hope he won't ask me to dinner. Why men can't be friends without bringing their wretched stomachs in is astounding. But, there you are. It's the ventral tube that governs the world.'

Willie leaned forwards towards me shyly. He spoke hesitantly.

'When you go out to work in the Congo, sir,' he said, 'could I come with you? I don't know the language or anything. But I could help somehow—if it was only looking after your kit. Could I go with you, sir?'

I felt a thrill of pleasure. For the first time in many months I was aware of a throbbing in my veins.

'Yes, Willie,' I said, 'you could go with me.'

Willie sprang up from his chair.

'Then I've got something to look forward to,' he said.

Suddenly a noise broke the stillness. I turned my head sharply in the direction of the river.

'What is it, sir?' asked Willie.

'Listen,' I said, and paused. 'I thought I heard the whistle of a steamer.'

I strode out on to the verandah. Willie followed me. He stood beside me expectantly while I gazed through the telescope. But I saw nothing. The only sound was the croaking of the bull-frogs. We walked back into the room.

As I poured us both another drink, Khalil came in and handed me a message form. I glanced briefly through it.

'Still not much news from our outposts,' I told Willie. 'A little sniping earlier, that's all.'

Khalil bowed and went out.

'Is he your head servant, sir?' Willie asked.

'Yes,' I replied. 'He's been in the Palace for nearly ten years.'

Willie glanced up at me and grinned.

'I bet *he* can give the girls a treat,' Willie said.

I pretended to be shocked, but, in fact, I was rather amused. I remembered now that when he was in high spirits, Willie had always been irrepressible.

'At present only three of them,' I answered solemnly.

Willie took a sip of his brandy.

''Course, they're allowed four wives, aren't they, sir?' he said. 'Fancy being nagged at by four women at a time. No wonder the men get old quickly. Funny people. But they're not bad when you get to know them. We had a guide with a long beard just like something out of the Bible. Do you remember that day when you took Miss Augusta's Scripture School—when you told us about David and the Giant, whatever his name was?'

I could remember the day well. I could also remember that I couldn't prevent myself glancing down, now and then, at the slim, fourteen-year old boy, in the second row of the class, with his black curly hair and heavy-lashed violet eyes.

'What ages ago it all seems,' I said.

'Well, you're like David now, sir,' Willie announced. 'With all those huge forces surrounding you.'

'Do you remember what I told you that day?' I asked him.

Willie screwed up his face in thought.

'You may be small like David,' he recited slowly, 'you may be all alone and people may jeer at you. But if in your heart you know you're right, then God will give you strength,' he paused. 'It's true, isn't it, sir?' he concluded.

'I believe so,' I answered.

'When I first saw you down at the docks that afternoon,' Willie said, 'if you'd told me you was a General, I'd of told you to go boil yourself.'

'Would you indeed,' I said, looking very stern.

"Course, I wouldn't say that now, sir,' Willie added quickly.

'I'm glad to hear it,' I answered.

'In the Army, when I told them I'd met you,' Willie said, 'they just wouldn't believe me. Do you know in England now you're as famous as Mr Gladstone? Well—almost.'

For once I found that I could laugh. I felt quite light-headed.

'It's strange,' I said. 'In ten or twelve years time Gladstone and Baring and I will have lost all our teeth and we'll be stone deaf. No one will come and court us in our clubs. New Barings and Gladstones will have arisen who'll call us "blokes" and "twaddlers". When we come into the club, some young Captain will nudge his friend and say: "Look, there's that dreadful bore coming in again. For goodness sake let's get away." It will be very humiliating—because all three of us think we're immortal.'

'So you will be, sir,' Willie said proudly. 'We're known as the Gordon Relief Expedition.'

'I wish it hadn't been called that, for it hasn't come to relieve *me*,' I told the boy. 'I'm not the rescued lamb and refuse to be. The expedition has come to save our national honour by doing for the Sudan what we promised.'

At that moment I was standing underneath the lantern by the open window, when a shell exploded close outside the Palace, sending up a spray of rubble on to the verandah.

'Oughtn't you to stand away from that window, sir?' Willie asked. 'I'm sure they're aiming for the light.'

'I'm certain they are,' I replied. 'But the range is two thousand two hundred yards. And as *we* never hit anything we fire at from that distance, I don't see why the Dervishes should either—so we're quite safe in the Palace. I'm far more worried about our last penny-steamer, moored outside.'

'What about snipers?' Willie asked.

'The bullet that kills you is marked with your initials,' I told him.

Willie gaped at me, then laughed. 'For a moment I didn't see what you meant,' he said.

As he spoke, once again I thought I heard a steamer's whistle. I went out on to the verandah. But there were still no lights on the river. In the silence the croaking of the bullfrogs seemed very loud. A damp stench came from the mudflats on the river's bank. I went back into the room. I longed to help myself to another drink, but I knew that with each drink I now took, desire would creep deeper into me.

I offered Willie a cigarette.

'Thanks, sir,' Willie said. Then he looked up at me and smiled. 'Do you know, I keep on forgetting you're a General,' he told me.

'Is that a compliment or not?' I asked.

'If you'd been a trooper in the British Army you'd know the answer to that one, sir,' Willie replied.

At that moment Khalil came in with a plate of food which he set before Willie. Khalil then bowed to me.

'Ya sidi, shall I clean out Colonel Stewart's room for the young effendi?' he asked.

I had known that Khalil was bound to ask that question sooner or later. I had been dreading it. Only I, myself, might know the implications of my answer. Colonel Stewart's room was at the far end of the Palace. If Willie slept in that room, then—to a certain extent—I had removed temptation from myself. But I had a valid excuse for telling Khalil to make up a bed for the boy in my own bedroom.

Then, at least, the welcome presence of his company would not be taken from me.

But as I gazed down at Willie, slender yet tough, sitting in his chair, smoking his cigarette, I felt a love so keen invading me that I had to turn away. I now felt almost faint. And I was afraid, I was afraid because I was aware that mixed with my love was a fierce desire.

If Willie slept in my room I might have to watch him taking off his clothes. I might have to contemplate the shape of the boy's limbs and the gracefulness of his body. And later, he would be lying naked in a bed only a few feet away from me.

If I put a few questions to the boy now I could discover if he were innocent or not.

If he weren't innocent, if I found that he shared my desire, would I then possess the strength of mind to resist—as I had always resisted before? My nerves, I was aware, were already worn; My will-power had already been extended to its limits. Did I have enough force left in my spirit to resist.

But even as I hesitated, Willie looked up at me and smiled. It was a smile of complicity.

I turned to Khalil and tried to speak briskly.

'You can put a bed for the young effendi in my room,' I told Khalil. 'I want him near me—not on the far side of the Palace. There may be fighting on the outposts tonight.'

Khalil bowed and left the room. He left us alone together.

It is now 3 a.m.

I have just been on to the roof to look through the telescope which I have permanently fixed there. There are no lights on the Nile.

I force myself to continue writing my journal in order to avoid thinking of the boy lying in my room next door.

At this moment, in twenty-four hours time, the steamers full of redcoats will arrive and Khartoum will be relieved. As a General and as a man of honour I rejoice. As a poor human-being my feelings are mixed. Part of me is aware that I must be grateful to God for preserving me from what might have been a terrible death, and for prolonging my existence. But another part of me is filled with a weariness and misery when I contemplate a future in which for many years to come my perpetual struggle against the evils of the flesh will continue. It may well be that the boy will be with me for each day in the Congo, so that on each day the struggle will be renewed.

If only I had a friend of my own age to whom I could confide my temptations and fears, perhaps they would be less intense. But, as it is, I am alone with my guilt, and the only escape-valve for my pent-up misery has been the act of writing these journals.

I destroyed each one of the journals I kept when I was in China because, when I read them through, I realised that they were too intimate and revealing. As a safety valve they had already served their purpose. This journal will certainly suffer the same fate. But I will take it with me to the Congo and re-read it in order to see if there is anything I can learn from its pages. Then I will destroy it.

I will not return to England. I told Kitchener this in a letter which I sent to him by one of my messengers two months ago. 'There will be no peace between me and Gladstone's Government,' I wrote to him. 'Neither will I accept anything whatsoever from them. And I will not let them pay my expenses. I will get the King of the Belgians to do so, and I will never set foot in England again.'

I like Sir Samuel Baker's description of Kitchener, which he wrote to me in a letter.

'The man whom I have always placed my hopes upon is Major Kitchener, R.E., who is one of the few *very superior* British officers, with a cool head and a hard constitution, combined with untiring energy.'

Whoever comes up here tomorrow with the Relief Expedition had better appoint Major Kitchener as Governor-General, for it is certain, after what has passed, that I am impossible. If Kitchener would take the place, he would be the best man to put in. But our Government must be prepared to renew the stores and war-material, and to give six thousand extra soldiers to the Sudan.

I have a great pity for these poor people of the Sudan. I would gladly give my life for them. How can I help feeling for them—however much they may have angered me at moments? All the time I have been here, every night I have prayed that God would lay upon me the burden of their sins and crush *me* with that burden, rather than these poor sheep around me. I have really wished and longed for it.

I may well be blamed for forcing an Expedition to be sent out here, by insisting on remaining in Khartoum. I am quite indifferent to whether I am blamed or not, for I feel I have only done—though poorly—my duty. The true facts will eventually be known. I do not mind the bitter words which may be said of me. There may even be an enquiry into my conduct. I do not care. They may say that I have sought after glory. That would be untrue. The fact is, as I've said before, if one analyses human glory, it is composed of 9/10 twaddle, perhaps 99/100 twaddle. For all I care, they may judge me or write about me as if I were dead, for, thank God, I am partially so with respect to what men say of me. I am certain that to undergo martyrdom, you have only to despise men's praise.

Since the day when I was as young as fourteen, I have asked myself why God should have chosen to inflict on me desires which—without breaking His Commandments—could never be fulfilled. Why cannot I love Willie Warren without a physical desire which can only soil the spirit of us both? I now know that I shall never be told the answer to this question until the day when I am released from the unclean envelope of flesh which I inhabit.

Meanwhile, the boy lies asleep in the room next door. The night is quiet. There are no calls of duty to distract me. So I must set down in this journal all that occurred in this room when Willie and I were left alone by Khalil a few hours ago.

After Khalil had left us there was silence for a moment. I had turned away from Willie, but I was very much aware that his violet eyes were watching me.

'What about a drink?' I asked him.

'Thanks, sir,' he answered. 'But only a small one. I mustn't get swimmy. I want to remember this evening.'

'You must have been in the ranks for quite a while,' I said to him as I poured out our drinks.

'Nearly a year, sir,' he answered.

'Are you happy?' I asked.

'Oh, happy as can be expected, you know, sir,' Willie replied.

I handed him his drink. 'Have you made any friends—close friends?' I asked Willie.

Willie stroked his cheek with his hand.

'I've got some mates,' he said. 'But none as I'd call close friends.'

'Why is that?' I asked gently.

'It's just not worked out that way,' Willie answered.

'That surprises me,' I said. 'And I seem to remember my sister Augusta telling me that you didn't make many friends in the school she'd sent you to before you joined up. But you're by no means a shy boy. So what's the explanation?'

Willie was staring straight ahead. Suddenly he looked sad. There was an odd bitterness in his voice when he spoke.

'Probably it's because I don't much take to people,' he said. 'And they don't take much to me.'

'Don't you sometimes feel lonely?' I asked him.

Willie began to rub the side of his face again. I noticed that the tip of his nose was peeling slightly from sun-burn.

'Yes,' he answered, 'sometimes.'

'I've felt lonely too at moments,' I said. 'In fact sometimes I feel that I've been lonely all my life.'

Willie gazed at me steadily. 'But after this, you won't be lonely any more—will you, sir?' he said. 'Because you promised just now that I could go to the Congo with you.'

I tried to smile. 'I wonder if you know what you'll be letting yourself in for?' I said.

Willie looked at me for a while in silence. His eyes were staring straight at mine. At that moment I felt almost sure that he must have understood the meaning implicit in my words.

'I've got a fair idea,' he answered quietly.

I knew that this was the time to ask him some question—the answer to which would tell me, once and for all, if his nature was in some way akin to mine. But I hesitated. Perhaps, because I couldn't bear the thought of being disappointed.

'Do your officers treat you well?' I asked him.

'Yes,' the boy answered. 'The officers are all right.' He

paused and took a sip of his drink. 'It's the N.C.O.'s who are the swine,' he added, 'or rather—some of them.'

Once again he had begun to rub the side of his left cheek.

'Do they take it out on you?' I asked.

Willie nodded.

'In what kind of way?' I enquired.

Willie looked down at his glass. 'You can guess, sir,' he answered. 'I'm sure you can. You see, sir, I'm the youngest in the troop.'

I went over to the table and filled my glass. My hands were shaky. The moment which I had at once dreaded and longed for was drawing close.

'Why don't you complain to your Troop-Leader?' I asked.

'He's all right,' Willie answered. 'He's a good soldier—I'll give him that. But, I don't think he'd know what I was talking about.'

'You seem to have learned a lot about life in this last year.'

'Yes,' Willie answered. 'But I knew most of it before.'

I was silent. His words made me realise just how little I really knew about the lives of the boys whom I had befriended. As I looked down at Willie's slender body, I could imagine what they might have done to him.

Then I shuddered in revulsion at the picture my imagination had produced. For suddenly I had glimpsed a scene in which a sergeant was treating Willie in the same way that Zubair had treated his little slave-boy in my vile nightmare. I could see the man's thick lips beneath his fair moustache. I could see his over-developed and hairy body. I could see his swollen face and his gross limbs. I picked up my glass and drank it down. I looked around at the solid furniture of the room in an effort to dispel the horrible image.

'Augusta told me that you did well at school. In fact, she wanted you to continue with your schooling. So why did you enlist?' I asked the boy.

'Because that's what you said I should do when I was old enough,' Willie answered.

At that instant, as I looked back over my life, I was appalled to think of the decisions I had taken so easily about the future of the boys who were temporarily in my care.

'But I didn't know then that you had the makings of a scholar,' I said.

Willie was still watching me intently. 'Well, it's too late now,' he replied.

'But you still haven't really answered my question,' I said. 'Why did you enlist?'

'Can't you guess, sir?' Willie asked.

I poured myself a drink. 'No,' I replied. 'I can't.'

'Do I have to tell you the real reason?' he asked me.

'Yes,' I answered quietly. 'I think you'll have to.'

Willie moved uncomfortably in his chair. He didn't speak. I pushed the tin of cigarettes towards him. He took one and lit it quickly.

'I'd have thought you'd have guessed the answer by now, sir,' he said. 'Enlisting was the only chance I'd got of ever seeing you again—if I was lucky.'

'I'm grateful to you Willie,' I said. 'But tell me, why were you sent here with Major Kitchener's message? Why was it you rather than some other, more experienced soldier?'

'P'rhaps because I'm a bit brighter than most of them,' Willie replied. 'Besides, I volunteered to come.'

'Did no others volunteer?' I asked.

'Dozens of 'em.' he answered.

'Then why did they choose you, Willie?' I repeated.

Willie had begun to stroke the side of his cheek again.

'P'rhaps because *he* hoped I wouldn't get through,' Willie answered. 'Reely I dunno.'

'Who's *he*?' I asked.

'The Sergeant-Major,' Willie replied.

'Why should that be his hope?' I asked.

Willie stared down at his cigarette.

'Because he had it in for me,' Willie answered.

'Why?'

'Because he'd taken to me,' Willie said. 'And I didn't want anything to do with him.'

I glanced out at the river. There were no lights. I could hear no sniping. It was completely still outside. I walked over to the map behind my desk and tried to concentrate on it for a while.

'Why did you want to see me again?' I asked.

I turned away from the map and glanced at him. Willie was still looking down at his hands.

'Why does anyone want to see someone again?' he asked.

I noticed that a strand of hair had fallen across his forehead.

'There could be various reasons,' I said.

Willie had almost finished his cigarette. The butt was so close to his fingers now that soon it must burn them. In the silence that followed Willie looked down at his right hand and became aware of this. He stretched out for the ashtray and stubbed it out. His gestures were short and vicious, as if he were crushing out some dangerous insect.

'Well, mine's quite simple,' Willie said.

I turned back to the map. 'Is it?' I asked. 'What?'

'I don't have to say, do I?' Willie said.

Then I knew for certain—beyond any doubt. For eleven months I had felt myself imprisoned in the Sudan. The prison had slowly become smaller. For the last month I had felt myself trapped in the Palace. I now felt myself a prisoner in far closer confinement. I felt that I was in an enclosure with Willie. An enclosure so small, that by moving my hand, I could touch him. And I was certain that this enclosure confined us both. My hands were shaking again. I clasped them behind my back. I knew that the words I spoke now might lead me towards the culmination of a danger that I had managed to avoid all my life. At the same time I was aware that I had no power left in me to control myself from uttering the words I knew might be fatal.

'So you won't mind sharing my room?' I asked.

Willie made no answer. He sat motionless, still gazing down at his hands. Outside I heard three shots of rifle-fire. Then, once more, the night was still, and I could hear the bull-frogs croaking in the mudflats of the Nile. Willie still did not move. His concentration on his scrutiny of his hands seemed so intense that I wondered if he had heard my question.

'So you won't mind?' I repeated.

Slowly Willie raised his head and looked up at me. Perhaps because I was standing so near to him, his eyes now seemed very large. The expression of his face was solemn, yet without any hint of strain or of embarrassment.

'I wouldn't have minded back in Southampton,' Willie said. 'After all, I gave you enough chances, didn't I?'

I looked at him, then swung round towards the verandah, and stood completely still. Small, unimportant little details of my recollections of this boy now came sliding back into my mind. I had turned away from him because I could feel the blood rising in my face. I could remember, now, the first time I had given him a bath. I could remember the involuntary movements he had made. I could remember, later that same night, when I put him to bed, that he had lain back on the mattress, parted his arms a little from his sides, and had remained thus, as if transfixed, watching me as if he were half-eager and half-afraid. I now realised that even in those days he had not been innocent. I put down my glass, I turned round and faced him. The strand of hair which had fallen across his forehead seemed to me to epitomise all my love for him and all my desire.

'Would you mind now?' I asked.

'No,' Willie said quietly.

'Is that what you want?' I asked.

When Willie looked up at me there was a kind of wonderment in his expression.

'Yes,' he answered. Then he paused. 'Now I've said it, haven't I?' he added.

His look of wonder still remained, but I perceived that to his wonderment was now added an element of enquiry and uncertainty. By this time my senses were so acutely atuned that I could understand the reason for his almost questioning look. It was because he could not understand the reasons which should make a man who has been his hero have desires which exactly matched his own.

'Come here,' I said to Willie.

Willie got up from his chair and moved towards me. Gently I raised my right hand and brushed back the strand of hair from across his forehead. The waves were sweeping over me now, but they were no longer waves of anger, and while they surged about me, I discovered that my spirit was rising away from the swirl and torrent into a harbour of calm, which was soon reaching a point of ecstasy. I leaned forward and kissed the smooth skin of his forehead that my right hand had laid bare. At first Willie did not move, but then I felt his hand touch mine.

'You realise this would be for good,' I heard myself say. 'Between us, I mean.'

Willie nodded, and I felt a peace, and for all that while I felt no stab of guilt. Indeed, I experienced a contentment and delight far beyond anything I had ever known. I was so sure that all would be well between us that I moved away a little. We stood watching each other, tranquilly, and I felt I had known the boy during every year of his life.

The door opened, and Khalil came in.

'The young effendi's bed is ready,' he announced.

'Thank you, Khalil,' I said.

Then I turned to Willie. In Khalil's presence I spoke briskly. 'You must be very tired,' I said. 'I suggest we should turn in.'

Then I turned back to Khalil. 'Good night,' I said. 'I'll be up at dawn as usual, but call me if there's anything of importance.'

Khalil bowed and left the room.

I opened the door that led into my bedroom. Willie followed me into the room. I showed him the bed Khalil had made up for him. Willie moved towards me and stood facing me. He was so close to me that I could feel the heat glowing from his body, and I could smell the odour that emanated from him. It was a pleasant smell—and rather reminded me of the smell of a young leopard cub I had once kept. He stood motionless with his arms raised a few inches from his sides, and with the palms of his hands facing me. Then I remembered it was the same attitude that he had adopted when I first put him to bed in our house in Southampton. He took a step forward. His body was now almost touching mine. The moment had come. I had only to put out an arm and draw him close to me. But I still hesitated. For some reason—perhaps because of my conscience—I suddenly became keenly aware of my position of responsibility, not only as a General with a trooper, but as an older man with a boy. I realised that if I allowed my emotion to reach any further with the boy I would in my own mind be accursed for ever.

'Willie,' I said gently, 'you must get into bed. I'll come back later, but I must make a tour of our defences first. It's very unlikely that the Mahdi will try to attack tonight, but I can't take the risk. I'll be back in about half an hour or so.

'Can't I come with you?' Willie asked.

'No,' I said. 'You're dog-tired and you must get some rest.'

'Can you stay for just a few minutes, sir?' Willie asked. 'Just till I'm in bed.'

'Very well,' I replied. I went and sat down on my own bed.

Willie slipped off his shirt. His neck and face had been sunburnt, but his chest, except for a deeply burned V where his shirt had been unbuttoned, was milk white. I could see that his skin was very smooth yet his body was finely muscled. Slowly he took off his breeches and lay naked on the top of his bed. The temptation was so strong that I felt a constriction round my chest so that I could hardly breathe. His limbs were perfectly made and his body was almost hairless. I had never seen such a beautiful form before. As I gazed down at him, I became aware of tremors of movement in his body.

'The night is cool,' I said, 'you'd better get into bed.'

Willie glanced up at me for an instant. Then he raised his legs and slipped them between the carefully folded-back cotton sheets. His smooth chest was still uncovered. I could see that his delicate shoulders sloped down to a surprisingly narrow waist.

Because I had felt the glow of heat from his body I knew how warm his skin would be to touch.

Willie smiled at me. 'I'll wait for you, sir,' he said. 'I'll stay awake until you come back.'

But I could see that his eyelids were already drooping.

'I won't be too long,' I said. 'But try and get some sleep.'

As I walked towards the door I stopped by his bed. 'Thank you for getting the message through to me,' I said. 'It's made all the difference.'

I put my hand lightly on his shoulder. His skin was so warm that I seemed to feel it almost burning against my hand. Then he began to tremble. He took my hand and began to slide it slowly down his chest. For a moment I let my hand be drawn downwards across his body. Then I summoned up the remaining force of will-power which was left in me and as gently as I could I withdrew my hand. Then I went over to my desk. I picked up the ledger book which contains this journal and left the room.

As I've said—I made my tour of the defences. Everywhere I went I found that the news that the British Expeditionary Force would arrive tomorrow had spread. The morale of my troops had changed from despair to elation. I made my tour last as long as possible because I dreaded returning to the Palace.

When I returned to this room—and when I was alone—I kneeled down and prayed to God to deliver me from temptation. Then, some strange voice in my head told me that so long as I kept writing in this journal I could retain my self-control. But I have drunk heavily, and my mind is confused.

I have put down in this journal all that occurred between Willie Warren and myself until this very moment. The boy is sleeping soundly in the room next door. But I know only too well that I've only to go into that room and touch his shoulder once again for him to draw me to him.

Therefore I must go on writing. And as I sit here odd, disconnected thoughts and remembrances from the past slip into my mind.

I remember how at Rockstone Place my sister would not allow me to smoke except in the kitchen. But I felt embarrassed by the cook and staff watching me, and they had only two afternoons off a week. So, in effect, my smoking was restricted to two afternoons a week, in the kitchen, throughout my stay there.

My sister Augusta would have made a wonderful wife for someone, but she never married. Maybe it is as well, for had she done so, I would have certainly lost a wonderful housekeeper.

I remember that a few days after Stead, the Editor of the *Pall Mall Gazette* visited me, we were called upon by a very pompous Equerry, who came with an invitation from 'His Royal Highness, The Prince of Wales,' who asked me 'to do him the honour of dining with him the following day.' But as I've said before, I had more important things to do than to fuss about with a Prince and the so-called smart society which surrounded him.

'Please offer His Royal Highness my humble respects and thanks,' I said, 'and my regrets that I shall be unable to accept his kind invitation.'

The pompous Equerry glared at me in astonishment. 'Perhaps I've not made myself clear,' he announced. 'The Prince of Wales *in person* invites you to dine with him tomorrow night.'

'Perhaps *I* have not made myself clear,' I replied. 'I regret *in person* that I am unable to accept.'

The Equerry looked outraged. 'But you cannot refuse the Prince of Wales,' he announced.

'Why not?' I asked, 'I once refused an Emperor—King John of Abyssinia—and he might have cut off my head for refusing.' I'd cast a sly look at Augusta. 'He even cut off the head of any of his subjects who was found smoking,' I said. 'I'm sure that His Royal Highness will not do that.'

'Then let me say you are ill,' the Equerry persisted.

'But I am not ill,' I replied.

The Equerry glared at me. 'I must insist that you give me some reason that I can give to the Prince.'

'Very well, then,' I said, 'tell him I always go to bed at half past nine.'

The Equerry gave a slight sniff of temper and walked out of the room. He had obviously decided that I was quite deranged. I've never tried to ingratiate myself with the powers and principalities of this world. Perhaps that is why I have so little experience of politicians.

I still do not understand the morality of Gladstone's Government. Why is it right to send an expedition *now* to relieve Khartoum, when it could have been too late, and not before? It is all very fine to consider the difficulties of the Government, but the feeling persists that they hoped it wouldn't be necessary to send an Expeditionary Force because Khartoum had fallen! I do not feel any particular rancour on the matter, but cannot admit to liking men such as those in the Government, who act in such a hypocritical way.

If a boy at an English school acted towards a fellow in a similar manner I think he would be kicked, and I am sure he would roundly deserve it.

I can think of no other parallel case in all of history, unless it be that of David and Uriah the Hittite. But then there was an Eve in the case, and I'm sure that no Eve exists here. Unless of course it be the Sudan, and I do not think that Great Britain wants to fight over *her*!

I do not, so much, judge the abandoning of the Garrisons —but I *do* judge the indecision of the Government. By their constant indecisiveness they have prevented me from taking up my post in the Congo and, until now, they have left me all but abandoned in Khartoum. This is my point of complaint.

Outside all is still quiet. I really have no excuse to visit my outposts again tonight, because it is quite certain that the Mahdi will not attack now. Moreover, by this time, some of his spies in Khartoum will have probably crossed over to tell him the news contained in Kitchener's letter. The Mahdi will realise that the morale of my troops has been restored.

The desire to go into my bedroom is almost overwhelming. As I sit here writing, drinking brandy and intensely fatigued, my mind keeps going back to think of Willie lying asleep in the next room.

If I keep writing I know I shall have the strength to sit

here—to fight off temptation. Dawn will not break for some time yet. Until that moment I must force myself to sit at this desk. At dawn Khalil and the other Palace servants will be about their business, and I will have no excuse to succumb to my temptation.

Why have I always had to fight against something stronger than myself? When I was a very small boy I used to give in to a sense of mischief. I was an ungodly boy. I would think nothing of making a dull Sunday afternoon lively by going around Woolwich, with my brothers, ringing all the door bells, and then running away. But at the back of my mind— as soon as I understood the nature of my desires—there was always guilt.

Then, when I was at Pembroke, as a young subaltern, I formed a friendship with a Captain Drew. This relationship with Drew has, I know, exerted a permanent influence on my life. He was a deeply religious man, and something about him caused me to change my occasionally sinful attitude towards prayer and worship. My feeling for God pleased dear Augusta, who for many years had been presenting me with volumes of sermons and religious thought. I had always laughed at them until I met Captain Drew.

I think it was my unhappiness, caused by those first exposures to military duties and the dreary round of social life, which led me towards God. Even in those days I found dinner-parties and social engagements so much boring jaw.

Perhaps I shall find happiness in the Congo. But ought I to allow Willie Warren to come with me? These days, though, I am afraid of solitude.

After Stewart and the others left, I wasn't quite alone. There was a rather swollen mouse which used to come and nibble at my plate at every meal. But I haven't seen her for some time now and I can't think what has happened to her. She made me feel less lonely.

I have just climbed up on to the roof to gaze through the big telescope. Though—as I expected—I could see nothing on the river. But as I stood there, a light breeze ruffled the waters of the Nile, and presently on the horizon to the East I could see that the light was coming back into the world. A few minutes later, as I stood there, I could see a faint streak of red above the minaret of the Mosque. I gazed at the desert beyond, and slowly, with layers and rivers of orange and scarlet and gold, dawn lifted itself from the desert around us, and soon the sun's rays reached Khartoum. In that moment, the drab assembly of dun-coloured mud-houses which make up Khartoum immediately became golden and magical. On the roof, I gazed around at the little domain that I still held. The Mahdi had proclaimed himself the Saviour of the Sudan. But I now knew that Khartoum would be relieved within twenty-four hours, and profoundly in my heart was inscribed the knowledge that if the Mahdi was the Saviour of the Sudan, so I was the Saviour of Khartoum. He had failed; I had succeeded.

Then, even as the vainglorious thought invaded my mind and I looked once more at the tides of dawn flooding the eastern sky with a hundred colours, I made myself forget my victory after a long siege. I caused my mind to descend below the roof—to my bedroom in which the boy was sleeping. And as I stretched out my arm to welcome the glory that God had sent on earth for another day, I knew that the freedom of spirit in my soul was allowed by God to enter there because—for all my longings and desires—I had kept untarnished the small temple of my body with which He had endowed me.

I was thankful that I had resisted both the forces without and the forces within.

The sky was now radiant with purple and shades of blue. The Dervishes had begun their sniping, but it seemed to me more half-hearted than usual. Obviously they had heard the news. Suddenly the timeless words came to me from the Scriptures. 'For what shall it profit a man, if he shall gain the whole world, and lose his own soul?'

I walked stiffly down the steps which led into my Operations Room. I felt more exhausted than I have ever felt in my life. But in my heart I felt that I might—during the recent hours—have won a victory, at least for a while, over the Devil who has oppressed me all the days of my life.

Now that dawn has come the Palace servants are awake. A period of temptation has temporarily gone.

Until my officers bring in their reports I will try to get some sleep on the leather sofa in this room.

Before I lie down to sleep, I will pray to God. Without vainglory, without any feeling that I have any claim to have my prayers granted, I will pray for my poor sheep in Khartoum. I will pray that, without desire, I may be able to have the fortitude to help the loneliness of those who—for the reasons of their nature, like Willie Warren—have found no friend. My last two prayers will be short. The first will be that during the next few crucial days I may have the strength to resist temptation. My last prayer will be for all of us. I will pray that those of us who are isolated in the tiny islands of our souls may awake to find ourselves joyful in a crowd.

As I've said, at fourteen I prayed to God to make me a eunuch. At seventeen, I began to pray for death. In the

Crimea, my prayer was almost granted. But since then I have tried to grow in wisdom. I have comprehended that I was placed in this world by God's will, and I must try to obey His commands. I must do God's will—as I see it—and I must avoid temptation until the day He sets me free.

Editor's Note

Khartoum was invaded by the Mahdi's forces at 3.30 a.m. on 26 January 1885. The invasion was successful. The two steamers, the *Bordein* and the *Talahawein*, which had linked up with the Gordon Relief Expedition reached Khartoum on January 28—two days too late. They were heavily bombarded from the Dervish gun emplacements at Omdurman. As they steered into the dark waters of the Blue Nile it was seen that no flag was flying, and that the Palace had been utterly destroyed. General Gordon had been killed. The steamers turned back and left Khartoum.

Trooper Warren's account, which now follows, shows the difference between the legend that was built up round Gordon's life—and the plain truth of the General's actions.

I have included it because I think it shows the strange— almost psychic—effect which General Gordon exercised on Warren's behaviour. His account also shows the fact that denial *or* indulgence can make the whole difference to a man's life and—in the General's case—to the fate of a whole country.

Trooper Warren's papers, letters and final testament, were all together in a small canvas bag. His last letter, dated 16 September 1885, was attached to the manilla envelope enclosing the ledger which contained General Gordon's last journal. This last letter from William Warren is written at some length. It completes General Gordon's journal and gives a first-hand account of what happened to the General during the last few hours of his life. It also describes what happened to Warren subsequently.

Both the journal and the letter were obviously suppressed by my aunt because of the nature of their contents. But, as I said in my foreword to this work, I have decided that the time has come when it should be published.

C. G. Luton

PART TWO

William Warren's Account

In the last frantic moments—which I'll write about later—the General gave me his journal. He ordered me to tear it up and then to chuck it into the Nile.

So when Bordeini Bey and I stumbled down the iron steps that led into the Palace garden, I stuffed the ledger inside the shirt I was wearing beneath my Dervish clothes. Bordeini knew a safe way down from the garden to the river. Vaguely, I was aware that Khalil was following us. Then we lost sight of him. We crept along the banks of the Blue Nile. Opposite Tuti Island, Bordeini had a small flat-bottomed boat tied up at a mooring. He unhooked the chain.

'Lie flat in the boat,' he said. 'Steer only with one paddle. The current will carry you downstream. Travel only by night. Hide by day where you can. You will find some food in a little sack in the boat. Stay on the Nile, there will always be water for you. In time you must reach the British forces or their steamers.'

Bordeini held out his hand. 'May Allah preserve you,' he said.

I began to try and thank him but he cut me short. 'If Allah so wills,' he said, 'we shall meet again.' Then he turned quickly away and left me.

I lay flat in the boat and pushed it off the mud with an oar. I soon learned the knack of steering it. When dawn came I made towards a clump of bushes on the right-hand bank. Using the oar, I managed to get the boat right beneath the bushes so no one could see her. Then I leaned over and had a long drink from the Nile. I was less frightened now. Presently I began to feel hungry. I untied the little sack. There were some biscuits in it and some sugar. I had nothing to do all day until sunset—except hope to God I wouldn't be found by the Dervishes. The ledger was still inside my shirt, pressing against me. I opened my shirt. I took out the ledger.

It was all I had left of the General. Really, I suppose I'd

enlisted just for him. In the hope that somehow or the other I'd get to see him again. I'd prayed to be posted to the Sudan in the Relief Expedition, and I'd succeeded. I'd actually reached Khartoum. Then, just when it seemed as if it was going to work out all right, the General was killed. I'd thought we'd be friends for years, after Khartoum had been relieved. I'd thought of my being with him in the Congo. But it all went wrong. I was on my own again, with no one in the world.

But I couldn't resist it—I couldn't resist having a read first. After all, it couldn't do the General any harm. Once I'd begun to read I didn't stop. I only prayed that the journal wouldn't end before the moment when I'd arrived at the Palace. For once in my life I got what I prayed for. I was in it all right. Very much so, in fact.

A few hours after dawn on the second day I'd fallen asleep at the bottom of my boat, underneath some overhanging bushes, and wrapped up in my Dervish robe, when suddenly I was awoken by rifle-fire near at hand. Cautiously I peered out from between the leaves of the bushes. Our two steamers were coming up the Nile towards Khartoum and the Dervishes were firing at them from the far bank. I didn't dare show myself for fear of being spotted, not only by the Dervishes but by some English sniper on board who might mistake me, in my stained smock, for one of the enemy— and shoot me. There was a chance that when the steamer's Commanders saw that Khartoum had fallen they would turn back. By then—with any luck—I'd have drifted past the outskirts of the Dervish forces and I could safely tear off my robe, and wave my hands to the steamers and shout at them in English.

And that's how it turned out. A boat was lowered from the Bordein to pick me up. By then I'd caught this rotten trouble with my lungs. I was coughing badly and found it difficult to breathe. I was in the ship's sick bay till we reached Korti.

My next of kin—or whoever reads this account of mine—may wonder why I didn't destroy the journal as the General had ordered me to do, before I was hauled on board the steamer or when we reached Korti. The reason was that, before I was rescued, I'd had time to read the journal through twice. For a while I hesitated. But when the moment came, and when we reached the safety of Korti, I felt I just couldn't give it up. I felt it belonged to me—if only because lots of it was something very personal to me, and I didn't want to get myself mixed up in a lot of awkward questioning. I'd already torn off the stiff covers of the ledger, so it wasn't difficult to hide.

I've said that I felt the journal belonged to me. Perhaps it was because I felt that in some strange way the General himself belonged to me—even though he was dead.

After all—he had invited me to go out alone with him, as his friend and companion, to fight slavery in the Congo. And even though we had never done anything together, I knew that he wanted me. I'd know it for certain on that first evening in Khartoum when he'd kissed my forehead. And later—when I lay on the bed in his little room—the awkward tense way he moved made me completely sure of it. But it wasn't just affection and lust. He really did love me. And in my own kind of way, I suppose I'd been in love with him ever since I saw him dressed in that shabby suit he always wore in England on that first night down at the docks in Southampton. It wasn't only that he was the first person who'd ever cared about me. I felt something about him that I simply can't quite explain. I wanted to give him everything I had in the world. I wanted to give *myself* to him. And I wanted to feel that in some way he belonged to me. I wanted to feel that he felt the same way about me as I felt about him. And I did find out—but too late.

Now he was dead and I was in the sick bay of a paddle-steamer on its way down the Nile.

When we reached Korti, I was put into the hospital and given some medicine to drink. I don't know what was in it, but it put me to sleep right till the following morning. When the orderly came in and began tidying me up, as if I was going on parade or something, I asked him what all the fuss was about. He told me the Chief Medical Officer was coming to see me. Presently a stout, red-faced Colonel came in, followed by two orderlies.

'How are you feeling, Warren?' the Colonel asked briskly.

'Better, sir,' I replied truthfully.

'I'm glad to hear it,' the old idiot replied. 'But *we* shall have to decide if you're better or not, shan't we?' And with that he whipped out a stethoscope and began listening to my chest and my back. Then he gave a little grunt.

'You'll do,' he said. 'Stay in bed all morning. This afternoon they'll fit you out with a clean uniform. Get yourself ready by five o'clock. You'll be wanted at Headquarters.'

I supposed they wanted to ask me a load of questions. They'd tried to question me when I was on the *Bordein*, but the Medical Officer there wouldn't let them. Anyhow, by that time I'd pretty well made up my mind as to what kind of answers I'd give them.

A sergeant and two corporals arrived as escorts on the dot at five o'clock. They marched me through the lines to Headquarters. They took me to the Intelligence Officer's quarters, which consisted of two tents, one small one and one large, both joined together.

I was marched into the smaller tent. On my right, at a desk made of wooden planks, sat a Captain who seemed to be writing out a series of telegraphs. He did not look up when we came in, so I had time to examine him. He had a broad forehead and a nose that sprang from his face like the figurehead of a ship. Beneath a close-clipped black moustache was a wide mouth so straight that you felt you could post a letter in it. If you'd taken a photograph of the top half of his face he'd have been a distinguished man. But below the pillar-box mouth his chin sloped straight downwards into the fleshy folds of his neck. After a pause, the sergeant stepped forward.

'Trooper Warren, sir,' he said, and gave a vigorous salute.

The Intelligence Officer looked up for a moment and his eyes slid towards me. Then he turned back to the sergeant.

'Thank you, Sergeant,' he said, 'you and your two corporals can dismiss. I shan't need you any more.'

The sergeant and the two corporals saluted smartly, turned on their heels and left.

The Intelligence Officer leaned forward on the desk, resting his chin on his left hand so that the weakness of it was hidden. 'I'd better explain all this rigmarole,' he said to me, sliding his mouth into a smile. I'm Captain Brownlow. I'm Major Kitchener's Deputy Intelligence Officer. We gather that you got through with Major Kitchener's message to the General. We also gather that you were in the Palace when the Mahdi's attack started. Is that correct?'

'Yes, sir,' I said.

'So you can see that we're interested to get your first-hand account of what happened.' the Captain said.

Then the Captain leaned forward still smiling at me from beneath his moustache. 'I should tell you,' he added, 'that it has been decided to recommend you for the Military Medal.' His smile slipped a bit. 'But the final decision on that may have to wait a while.'

As the Captain spoke I glanced into the large tent which was linked to the smaller one by the canvas being rolled back to form a sort of V-shaped entrance. The man seated at the desk in the large tent was hidden from my view. But the evening sun was slanting through the side of the tent so that I could see the man in profile. He was sitting motionless. He was very thin. His back was straight as a ramrod. Even before I saw the outline of the outsized moustache I guessed it was Major Kitchener. For I had seen him several times on parade.

The Captain was now pushing a tin of cigarettes towards me. 'Sit down,' he said to me, 'and light up. This isn't a drill inspection, you know.' He gave a small laugh.

I sat down on the canvas chair opposite the desk. I lit my cigarette and tried to appear at ease. It was hard for me, because I was beginning to feel groggy again.

'Now then,' the Captain began in a deliberately gentle tone of voice, 'I just want you to answer me a few simple questions. First, on what day and at what hour did you arrive at the Palace in Khartoum?'

'Soon after midnight, sir, on January 24th,' I replied.

The Captain made a note on the foolscap pad in front of him.

'And you handed Major Kitchener's letter to the General?'

'No, sir,' I answered. 'I gave it to Khalil, who was the General's head servant in the Palace.'

The Captain made another note. 'And later you were summoned into the General's presence?' he asked.

'Yes, sir,' I answered. 'I was waiting downstairs. He sent the servant to fetch me.'

'I expect the General was glad to see a white face again after all that time?' the Captain asked.

'Yes, sir,' I answered.

The Captain now looked down at another foolscap pad which was lying close to his left elbow.

'We've heard from some of the men in your regiment

that you once claimed you'd met General Gordon before you enlisted,' he said. 'Is that true?'

I glanced up at the main tent and it seemed to me that the outline I could see through the tent flap stiffened. But at that stage I wasn't alarmed. I'd thought out ways of answering his questions, sticking as close to the truth as I could without giving away my secret.

'Yes, sir,' I answered. 'When I was in Southampton I met the General and his sister, Miss Augusta. I'd got no work, and I'd run away from home. Miss Augusta sent me to school.'

Captain Brownlow was now watching me very carefully.

'Did General Gordon recognise you when you appeared in his room in the Palace?' he asked.

'Not at first, he didn't,' I replied. 'But after I'd been there a few minutes, he did.'

'That was in the main room of the Palace, was it not?' the Captain asked.

'Yes, sir.'

'So I expect you stayed there talking with the General for quite a while?'

'Yes, sir,' I answered. 'I did.'

'How long did you stay with him?'

'About an hour,' I answered.

The Captain looked surprised. 'An hour!' he exclaimed. 'That's quite a long time. What did you talk about?' His eyes were now fixed on me.

I looked straight back at him. 'The General wanted to find out all he could about the Relief Expedition,' I replied.

The Captain began playing with his pencil. 'But by then, you must have been very tired,' he said in a rather vague tone of voice.

'Yes, sir, I was,' I replied promptly. The Captain was still fiddling with his pencil, rolling it between his pudgy fingers.

'So after your talk with the General,' he said, 'I expect you went to bed.'

'Yes, sir,' I answered.

'I suppose there were plenty of rooms available in the Palace,' Captain Brownlow said.

'Yes, sir,' I answered.

'So in which room did you sleep?' he asked me.

I could see that the figure behind the tent-flap had half turned in our direction.

'It was in a room at the far end of the Palace,' I answered. 'I think it was the room where Colonel Stewart used to sleep.'

For a second a flicker of surprise showed in the Captain's face. Once again, he looked down at the foolscap pad by his left elbow. I could see there were some pencilled notes scribbled on it. At that moment I was almost certain that my story of those last two nights in the Palace was being checked against someone else's account of them. But whose? It couldn't be Bordeini Bey. He'd made complicated arrangements to stay behind. Perhaps it was Khalil. I realised now that I must be very cautious.

'So you slept in Colonel Stewart's old room,' the Captain said. 'And you were there alone I take it?'

'Yes, sir,' I replied.

'At what hour did you wake up?'

'No one came to wake me,' I explained, 'and I was so tired that I slept on till about noon when I was woken by the sniping that was going on.'

'When did you next see General Gordon?' the Captain asked.

'When I got up and dressed, I found he'd gone out to inspect his defences,' I answered truthfully. 'Khalil brought me something to eat. That afternoon I wanted to join the General at the outposts. But Khalil told me that the General had left orders for me to stay in the Palace and rest. I expect he didn't want me in his way,' I added.

'But the General must have returned to the Palace at some moment during that evening,' the Captain said.

'Yes, he did,' I answered. Then I told another cautious lie. 'But he shut himself up in his room and wouldn't see anybody,' I added.

'So when, in fact, did you next see the General?' the Captain asked.

'He came in for a moment and had supper in the main room—the one he called his Operations Room,' I said. 'Immediately after that he went out again. He gave me orders to go to my room and get some sleep because he expected the Expeditionary Force would be arriving some time between midnight and dawn.'

'So you went back to Colonel Stewart's old room?' Captain Brownlow asked.

'Yes, sir,' I replied. 'About 3 a.m. I was woken up by heavy rifle-fire. I got up and went along to the Operations Room. Khalil told me the General was still on the roof looking through the big telescope. I went to the smaller telescope on the verandah. But I couldn't see any lights on the Nile. When I went back into the Operations Room General Gordon was there, studying the map of his defences. At that moment Khalil came up and told him that Bordeini Bey, the merchant, was downstairs and wished to see him urgently. The General gave instructions for Bordeini to be shown up. When Bordeini came in, I could see from his face that something terrible had happened.'

'What did Bordeini say?' the Captain asked.

'He told the General that the steamer *Bordein* had run aground by the head of the last rapids. He said that the *Talahawein* had stayed behind to help her.'

'And you were present at that moment?'

'Yes, sir.'

'Can you tell me how General Gordon reacted to this news?' the Captain asked me.

By now I had realised that my safest plan was to give them the kind of answers they'd *want* to hear.

'He took the news calmly,' I said. 'He realised that if the

White Nile was low enough for the Dervishes to cross, the Mahdi's forces would attack almost immediately.'

'Did the General give you any instructions?' the Captain asked.

'Yes, sir,' I replied. 'He told me to put on the Dervish smock that I'd arrived in and to make my way back to our lines as best I could. He told me to wait until the main attack started and to make my escape then.'

'Why?' Captain Brownlow asked.

'Because he knew that the main Dervish force would storm the Palace gates,' I answered. 'He knew they'd make for the main room of the Palace once they'd got in. In the meantime, Bordeini and I would have a good chance of getting down from the verandah into the garden and on to the Nile.'

'But Bordeini didn't escape with you,' the Captain remarked.

'No, sir,' I answered. 'He'd worked things out so that he'd be safe if he stayed behind.'

I noticed he didn't ask me about Khalil. I was now sure that my guess had been right. Khalil had somehow reached Korti.

'Will you now please tell me in your own words what happened?' Captain Brownlow asked.

'There was a bright moon that night,' I said. 'The Dervishes must have somehow crept forward beneath the ramparts. They must have opened fire at quite short range. They must have got in through the South West Gate. From then on it was pure bedlam. The Dervishes swarmed into the Palace Gardens at the front. Bordeini and I had gone out on to the verandah, close to the iron steps. But we could still see into the main room. The General told us to wait until he opened the main door on to the stairs . . .'

'Did you realise what would happen when he opened that door?' the Captain asked me.

'Yes,' I replied. 'But he wouldn't listen, not even to Bordeini Bey.'

'So you saw the final triumphant moment of the General's life?' Captain Brownlow asked.

I could see the figure in the tent next door was tense and listening.

'Yes, sir,' I answered. 'I saw the General fling open the main door. A howling mass of Dervishes rushed towards him. The General did not move from the head of the staircase. He stood there like a rock. Then he raised his right hand. A Dervish rushed forward with a shriek and plunged his spear into the General's heart.'

For a moment Captain Brownlow looked down at his desk and was silent. He began to fiddle with the pencils, pens and inkpots on it. I could see that he was genuinely moved.

'General Gordon was a great man,' he said in a curiously soft voice. Then he clamped his left hand back into position to hide his chin and stared up at me. 'Can you describe for me the General's attitude when he raised his right arm—you must have had some kind of sideways view I presume? Could you say he raised his arm in a gesture of disdain?'

This was obviously the answer he wanted.

'Yes, sir,' I replied. 'He raised his arm in a gesture of disdain.'

The Captain leaned forward. He'd recovered from his moment of emotion. He was cool and alert once more.

'When the attack started and the General gave you his orders to try to make your way back to our lines,' he said, 'did he give you any letter or message in writing?'

It's not right to say that when people are telling the truth they always stare you straight in the face. I know this and I'm sure Captain Brownlow did too. So when I told my lie, I told it quite casually, without fixing my eyes on him.

'No, sir,' I said. 'The General didn't give me any document.'

Captain Brownlow looked at me in silence for a while.

'I find that rather surprising,' he said. 'I would have thought that at least he would have given you a despatch.'

'I don't think the General expected the Dervish attack to come so quickly,' I said. 'Once they'd broken in, there just wasn't time for him to write anything.'

The Captain was still watching me carefully. His eyes, I noticed, had white rings around their centre—like a parrot.

'What clothes was the General wearing?' he asked suddenly.

I saw the trap in time. He must have been told the truth by Khalil.

'The General went to his bedroom and changed into his full-dress white uniform,' I answered.

'So he had time to do that,' the Captain commented.

'Yes, sir,' I answered.

'Yet he didn't have time to write a despatch. It's curious, isn't it?' the Captain said.

I was silent. The strange, parrot eyes were now examining me as if I were some message in code that he'd got to decipher. Suddenly, I began coughing. I just couldn't stop myself. I took out my handkerchief and put it to my mouth. I was almost choking. Captain Brownlow waited patiently until my coughing fit was over.

'Did the General give you any message?' he asked.

I decided to play it safe. I remembered a line from the journal. 'Yes, sir,' I answered. 'He did.'

'Then what was it?' the Captain asked.

I spoke slowly as I remembered the words the General had written in the journal. 'Tell them that I have done the best for the honour of our country,' I said.

Captain Brownlow wrote down the words on his foolscap pad. Then he looked up at me again. He now appeared satisfied with me.

'When you get back to your regiment tonight,' he said, 'I expect they'll ask you quite a lot about the time you spent with the General. I hope your answers will be as truthful and as brief as they've been to me.'

Suddenly the figure I could see through the tent-flap rose from his desk and appeared in the entrance to the tent we were sitting in. He stood framed by the opening. His face had grown more p rple since I'd last seen him, and his moustache had definitely grown larger. I got up and sprang to attention. Major Kitchener walked slowly towards me. In his right hand he was holding a small medal-ribbon.

'Trooper Warren,' Major Kitchener said, stretching out his right hand, 'it gives me pleasure to pin the ribbon of the Military Medal on your chest. You've deserved it. I want to add just a few words to those which my friend Captain Brownlow has said to you already. When you get back to your regiment this evening, I want you to tell them the exact truth as we've heard it today. You can tell them that you were one of the volunteers who was given a copy of my message to get through to General Gordon in Khartoum. You can tell them you were the only one to get through. You can tell them that the General arranged for you to be installed in Colonel Stewart's former room. And you can tell them you were privileged to spend the last few minutes of General Gordon's life in his presence.'

For a moment he paused. Of course, I saw what he was getting at. Khalil must have told them that I'd shared the General's bedroom. Both Major Kitchener and Captain Brownlow must have been delighted by the lie I'd told about sleeping at the far end of the Palace. I suppose they must have put it down to some shyness or even to some shame on my part. My lie had helped them to keep up the hypocrisy. It was obvious that the General had become overnight the most famous hero in England. So they were determined to present him to the troops, and to the world, as a man without a single stain or smear on his character.

Kitchener jerked his head back suddenly, as if he'd just remembered something. 'My Chief Medical Officer informs me that there's something wrong with your lungs,' he said. 'I've arranged for you to leave with some transport that I'm sending back to Cairo tomorrow morning.'

Then he nodded his head at me, turned around and went back into the main tent. Captain Brownlow got up from his desk. My interrogation was over. I saluted and left the tent.

On my way back to my regiment's lines, I was not surprised to see Khalil (outside the Officers' Mess). He was squatting on a mat outside the tent rather lazily polishing some silver. When he looked up and recognised me, he got to his feet and moved forward to greet me. There was no sign of embarrassment in his attitude. Obviously—in his mind—he had done nothing wrong. Obviously, to him, Gordon's attitude towards his servants and the soldiers who served under him at Khartoum had been completely correct. However, it now struck me that he must have noticed that the General's bed, on the first night that I spent in the Palace, had not been slept in. Perhaps the General used quite often to sleep on the leather-covered couch in the Operations Room. Then again, maybe he never had before. I would never know.

I was in a hurry to get back to our lines, but I listened to Khalil's story of his escape from Khartoum and of his managing to attract the attention of one of the small boats accompanying the *Talahawein*. But while I listened to him the pain in my chest grew worse. I made an excuse to leave him.

Major Kitchener and Captain Brownlow needn't have worried about my blabbing when I talked about my adventures to my mates in the regiment. By the time I reached our lines in the camp I was so ill again that I was put to bed.

The Military Hospital in Cairo was overcrowded and under-staffed. Those who were strong enough to move had to lend a hand in helping the orderlies look after those who were really sick. I was glad when I was well enough—or seemed well enough—to be transferred to the Sick Leave camp.

One afternoon, a week later, there was a Sick Parade. In the hot sunshine, we stood outside the Medical Officer's tent. By persuasion, and by a little cunning, I'd managed to be sixth in the queue.

When I got into the tent the Chief Medical Officer asked me to strip. He examined me all over for crabs or lice or venereal disease. Then he glanced at my medical chart. He took out his stethoscope and made me take deep breaths in and out. He listened to my chest and to my back longer than he'd ever done before.

When he'd finished he looked grim. 'You won't do,' he said. 'We can't treat you here. You'll have to be invalided home.'

Hurriedly he wrote out a chit. 'Give this to the Camp Adjutant,' he said. 'He'll make the necessary arrangements.'

The sick bay of the ship is crammed. But they've given me a top bunk near to the ventilation pipe, so at least I can breathe, and I'm well out of the way of the rest of them.

Before I left Cairo I managed to scrounge a supply of writing paper—enough to finish this long letter of mine. And I'm now determined to finish it—for two reasons. First because the laborious work of writing it all down helps me to stop thinking about the best friend of my life—dead in Khartoum. Secondly, because the record's still not complete, and I believe it deserves to see the light of day.

In case I would croak out before the ship reaches Southampton, my next of kin will probably be my sister Maude. Anyhow—whoever he or she may be that comes to open this packet, and begins to read these pages I've written, will be very shocked, I'm sure of it. But it's hypocrisy that keeps the world from knowing the truth about hundreds more people than you'd ever guess about. Even so, I'm afraid I'll be thought of by my relations as some kind of unnatural freak. They'll think so—till they come to read the General's journal written in the ledger which I've enclosed in this packet together with the pages I've written. They'll notice, at the same time, that there's a significant gap at the end of General Gordon's journal. Let me explain. The General's last entry in his journal was made at dawn on the morning of 25 January. But when I got back to our lines at Korti and was interrogated by Captain Brownlow, I made a point of only speaking about what the General had done that night which concerned his military command. As I've said, I told several lies about that fatal night of 25 January. I said I went to bed. I said I only woke up when the invasion started at 3 a.m. on the morning of 26 January.

So the record's incomplete. Before I seal up this packet, and while my memory's still fresh, I shall complete the record and fill in the gap.

On that evening of 25 January in the Palace in Khartoum, Khalil tapped on my door and said that supper was ready. The General was already seated at the table. I hadn't seen him all day. He greeted me briefly and then went on with his meal. There was a bottle of wine on the table. Khalil poured me out a glass. I drank it down quickly to give me confidence. I knew I had to ask the question that had been plaguing me all day. I took a deep breath.

'Excuse me, sir,' I began, 'can I ask you something?'

The General glanced up at me sharply. 'Yes,' he answered. 'What is it?'

'Last night, sir,' I said 'you said you were coming back to your own bedroom. But you never did come back.'

'I had work to do,' the General answered. 'I had to inspect

my fortifications. Then I had to write up my journal.' He pointed to the ledger which was lying on his desk.

Khalil had refilled my glass. I took another gulp of wine.

'Khalil told me you came back towards dawn, sir. You lay down for a while on the leather sofa in this room,' I said.

'Yes,' the General answered. Then his hectic eyes glared at me. 'I must also add that I think you should know better than to interrogate my servants as to my movements.'

The General finished his glass of wine, wiped his mouth with his napkin and rose from the table.

'I'll see you later,' he said to me. 'I expect the Expeditionary Force to arrive within six hours. I'd like you to be in this room so you can run various messages for me.'

He walked towards the door. Back in England, his step had been light. But now he dragged his feet heavily behind him. He opened the door, then turned back to me.

'You must forgive me, Willie,' he said—and for the first time I noticed that his voice was a little slurred. 'But these last few days have been a terrible ordeal for me. I'm afraid my nerves make me surly and difficult to get on with.'

Then he left the room.

I finished my meal. I left the table and lay down on the leather sofa.

At two in the morning the General walked into the room. I got to my feet. The General crossed to the drinks-tray and poured himself a glass of neat brandy. I saw that his hands were shaking, as if he were in a fever.

'For the last half an hour I've been on the roof, watching through the big telescope,' he told me. 'There's not a sign of any lights on the Nile. What in heaven's name can have happened? The message said they would be here by three this morning.'

Suddenly Khalil came in. 'Bordeini Bey is downstairs to see you, ya sidi,' he announced.

'Show him up,' the General said. Then he returned to me. 'Help yourself to a drink,' he said. 'I have a presentiment we're going to need all the drink we can get before this night is out.'

A few minutes later Bordeini Bey walked in. I'd never seen him before, and he looked rather like a clown at the circus to me. His face was very pale. His clothes seemed to be five sizes too big for him.

'Bordeini,' the General said. 'I want you to meet my friend Willie Warren.'

I moved forward and shook hands with the odd-looking man.

'What brings you at this late hour, Bordeini?' the General asked him.

Then, through his bloodshot eyes he saw the expression on Bordeini's face. 'What is it?' he asked. 'Quickly, speak, man.'

'One of the men we sent out to spy yesterday is come back to our lines,' Bordeini began. His voice was tremulous. For a moment he stared down in silence at the carpet on the floor. 'The man travelled far down the river,' he continued. 'Always he is watching the river. Soon, he sees two steamers coming. The *Bordein* comes first, then the *Talaha-wein*. Both have redcoats on board.' His voice faltered and he stopped. Bordeini's hands were plucking nervously at his embroidered waistcoat. I felt he was very near to collapse.

The General poured out a glass of brandy and gave it to him.

'What is it you're trying to tell me?' the General asked quietly.

Bordeini lowered his head till he was gazing at a pattern in the carpet only a few feet away from him.

'The steamer *Bordein* is aground,' he said.

The General was silent. His hands were shaking again. He clasped them together behind his back. 'What time was that?' he asked.

'Near sunset,' Bordeini answered.

The General glanced down at his watch. 'Nine hours ago,' he said. 'Where did she run aground?'

'By the head of the last rapids,' Bordeini replied.

For an instant a look of wild terror flickered across the General's face. He began to tremble. Suddenly he slapped his hand down on the desk. 'Impossible!' he cried. 'They must have got further than that.'

'I know this man who is our agent,' Bordeini answered. 'Always he is honest.'

'What of the other steamer?' the General asked.

Bordeini's jowls wobbled. Slowly he raised his head and looked towards the General.

'The *Talahawein* stayed behind to help the *Bordein*,' he said.

The General stared at Bordeini. At that moment his large blue eyes had a look of frightening madness in them. 'She stayed behind?' he asked. 'You're sure?'

Bordeini nodded his head. 'Yes, Excellency,' he answered.

With one quick movement of his hand the General raised his glass to his lips and drained it. When he spoke now, his voice was terrible in its tone of complete defeat.

Slowly he dragged his feet towards the window. He looked out at the Nile for a while in silence. Then he turned back to the two of us in the room.

'Then the game is up,' he said.

Frantically the General beat his fists against his forehead. He looked up at us. His face was mottled.

'I told them that a handful of Redcoats was all I needed,' he shouted. 'Why couldn't they believe me? One steamer alone would have done the trick. The fools, the fools. They'll arrive too late.'

'But, Excellency,' Bordeini began.

The General wasn't even listening to him. 'It may be two days—even three days now—before they arrive,' he cried out in a kind of moan of despair. 'Why couldn't they listen to me?'

'There is still hope,' Bordeini said. 'Perhaps in small boats . . .'

The General helped himself to another drink. 'Perhaps, perhaps,' he muttered.

It was ghastly to see his despair. As I looked at him I noticed for the first time that there were wine stains on his open shirt and down the sides of the white trousers of his uniform.

'I shall keep the news secret,' Bordeini told him. I knew he was trying to keep a quavering note from his voice. 'The agent is my friend. He will tell no one.'

The General made an effort to control his anger and despair. 'Thank you, Bordeini,' he said. 'You have done your best. You look exhausted. Help yourself to another drink. There's nothing we can do now except wait—as if I haven't waited long enough already.'

I felt a great yearning to help the General in his hour of need. 'Can't I do something, sir?' I asked.

The General turned round to look at me. It was quite obvious that in his excitement and rage he had completely forgotten my presence. For an instant he stared at me blankly. At the time I was hurt that he wasn't even aware that I was in the room. But I think I can understand it now. You see, when he'd been alone with me that first night it had been the man—the true man who had spoken to me. But now the General had taken over completely.

'Yes, work out with Bordeini some plan for getting yourself back to the English lines so that you can tell them what's happened,' the General said.

'I'm not leaving, sir,' I replied.

'You'll do as you're told,' the General ordered.

Then he walked on to the verandah to look through his telescope. I was left alone with Bordeini. I had got used to the sound of the firing, but it now seemed much closer. Bordeini crossed the room towards me.

'Are you the soldier who brought His Excellency the message?' he asked.

'That's right,' I answered.

Bordeini shook my hand. 'I'm glad to meet you,' he said. 'You must be very brave.'

'I don't know about that,' I answered. 'I just wanted to get through to him—that's all.'

At that moment the General came in from the verandah. His face was grim.

'Bordeini, can you take Willie with you?' he asked.

'Yes,' Bordeini replied. 'If he will wear the Dervish clothes he wore when he came here—Khalil tells me he's put them in a cupboard here. Also, he must do exactly what I say.'

The General turned to me. 'You will follow Bordeini's instructions until you get through the Dervish lines,' he said. 'Then you will rejoin the British Forces as best you can.'

'Can't I stay, sir?' I asked.

'And be murdered in this Palace?' the General answered. 'No, Willie.'

Once again the General walked out on to the verandah.

'Is it true?' I asked Bordeini. 'Isn't there a chance we can hold the Dervishes at least for a time?'

'Our men are so weak they cannot even move,' Bordeini answered. 'They can only stand at their posts.'

'Couldn't we hold them even for a day?' I asked.

'No,' Bordeini replied. 'Every Dervish who breaks through will run towards this Palace. If they break through, within ten minutes every man left in this Palace will be dead. We have few servants to defend it. If only the General would come with us, he might still escape.'

As Bordeini spoke there was a sound of general rifle-fire, and shells began to drop on all sides of us. I looked through the windows. The darkness of the night was pierced by the glow of torches. Very faintly, in the distance, we could hear the war-cries of the Dervishes. The attack had started.

Bordeini was standing beside me at the open window.

'There are many thousand torches,' he said quietly. 'The Mahdi is attacking with all his people. But our men are firing back quick enough.'

Khalil came into the room as the General hurried in from the verandah. The General looked pale. His face was horribly distressed.

'They're attacking the whole way along the line,' he said. He turned to Khalil. 'Send a runner to Faregh Pasha,' he said. 'Tell him the main attack is coming from Kala Kala on the White Nile end.'

Then the General turned to Bordeini and me. 'Get out while you can,' he said.

'No, Excellency,' Bordeini answered. 'We must wait. We cannot get through until they are attacking.'

'And if they break through our lines?' the General asked.

'Then there will be confusion,' Bordeini replied, 'and I can help the boy to escape.'

'Do as you think best,' the General said. He crossed to the desk and glanced up to the map of the defences.

'Isn't there anything I can do to help?' I asked.

'You can do what Bordeini tells you,' the General answered abruptly. 'There's precious little any of us can do. Except wait. God help us.'

The General went back quickly to the verandah. Bordeini moved close to me. 'When the time is come to go,' he said, 'follow me along the verandah. At the far end are steps down to the garden. We go north for a little and we meet the Nile. I will guide you from there. Move a few paces behind me—as if you were my servant. If they stop me, do not speak.'

'Thank you, sir,' I said.

Bordeini looked at me in surprise. 'You call me "sir",' he said.

'Aren't you a "sir"?' I asked.

'Yes, I am a Bey,' Bordeini answered. 'But I never expected an Englishman to call me "sir".'

'Why's that?' I asked.

'Because my skin is not white,' Bordeini said.

The noise of the rifle-fire was drawing closer. We could hear the shrieks of our men as they were shot or speared to death by the Dervishes. The sound of those wild fanatics, baying like hounds for lust and blood was very terrible.

'Go to the window and look,' Bordeini told me. 'I am too much afraid.'

I gazed out. The moon was now bright in a clear sky, but below there was dust and confusion.

'Their torches are coming closer,' I told Bordeini.

'May Allah preserve us,' he whispered.

For a moment there was silence. Then, slowly, with heavy dragging steps, the General walked in from the verandah. He looked like an old man. He was shaking as if from palsy.

'Not all the might of Britain can save us now,' he said.

He walked slowly to the drinks-table and poured himself a brandy. 'Close the windows,' he said to me. 'We'll hear their din soon enough.'

Suddenly his face was contorted with bitterness.

'It took them four months to make up their minds to send an Expeditionary Force,' he said. 'Even when they'd left Cairo, it took them three months to reach Metemma. I could have reached it in three weeks. Now they'll arrive too late.'

He drained his glass and flung it down to smash on the floor. 'God curse them!' he shrieked out. 'God curse them!'

He looked up and saw the two of us watching him.

'Well?' he asked. 'What are you waiting for?'

'Get the clothes you came in,' Bordeini said to me quietly. 'Put them on. We can leave soon.'

I went to the cupboard where Khalil had flung the clothes I'd come in that night which now seemed so very long ago.

Bordeini walked up to the General. 'Goodbye, General Gordon,' he said.

The General stared at him vacantly. 'Goodbye, Bordeini,' he muttered. 'Thank you for your help.'

Bordeini turned away quickly.

'Are you ready?' he asked me.

'Yes,' I answered.

I went up to the General. 'Goodbye, sir,' I said.

The General would not look at me. 'Goodbye, Willie,' he answered absent-mindedly. 'Good luck.'

But after all that had happened I couldn't just be dismissed like that. If I'd got to live without him for the rest of my life, I needed him to give me at least some strength or some hope to live for.

'The words are still true,' I said hesitantly, 'aren't they, sir?'

The General had lit a cigarette and his eyes were fixed on its glowing tip. 'The words,' he repeated vaguely.

I was afraid now. I had an instinct that if I quoted the words it would remind him of something he very much wanted to forget. But I'd gone too far. It was too late to stop myself.

'If in your heart you know you're right,' I quoted, mumbling the words from nervousness, 'then God will give you strength.'

The General stared at me. He began to tremble. His face was twisted as if he were having a stroke. He took a step towards me. For an instant I thought he was going to strike me. But he stood there, glaring at me. He was breathing heavily. Then I saw the blood rushing to his face.

'You impudent little fool,' he shouted at me. 'You trumped-up little guttersnipe. What do you know of strength? What do you know of defeat? What do you know of temptation? Do as you're told—and get out! For God's sake leave me alone.'

Then he stumbled towards the door that led to his bedroom. The door slammed behind him. I stared after him. I knew that tears of humiliation had come into my eyes. I couldn't help it.

Bordeini spoke very gently. 'You must understand,' he said, 'he has suffered too much.'

Slowly I began to put on my Dervish clothes. But each moment now the thought was beating in my mind—he didn't mean the words he told me to remember. He never meant what he said to me. He didn't mean any of it.

Bordeini went to the window and looked out. Then he lowered the lantern that hung over the desk and blew out the candles, one by one. The only light now burning was a small lamp on the desk.

'Are you ready?' Bordeini asked me. 'Soon it will be time to go.'

I nodded my head. My mind was full of agony. What's the point of it—I was thinking. All I can do now is to go back to where I was before I met him. I'd never have stuck the Army if it hadn't been for him. I'd be in irons by now. What's the point of it? I'm nobody. I've got nothing to look forward to. There's not a soul in the whole bloody world gives a rap if I live or die.

I went to the drinks-table and poured out a glass of brandy for Bordeini and myself.

'Thank you,' Bordeini said. Then he looked at me for a while in silence. 'You have been hurt,' he said. 'At this moment you think that life is not worth living. But you are young. You will live. You will forget.'

I tried to thank him, but I found I couldn't speak. Bordeini was now standing with his eyes fixed on the door to the General's room. Suddenly I saw him gape in astonishment at something behind me.

I turned round. The door was open, and the General was

standing in the doorway. Above his stained white trousers, he had put on the tunic jacket of his full-dress white uniform. The rows of medals on his chest glittered in the lamplight. There was a sword at his belt. But it was not the uniform that surprised me. It was the change that I could see in the General. This change was so great that for a second I wondered if it was a different person. Then I saw the familiar lines of the face I'd carried in my mind for so long. But—from his appearance only a few minutes previously—his whole countenance and bearing had been transformed. All bitterness and despair had vanished from his face. He now seemed in complete control of himself. His expression was at once radiant and serene. He held himself very erect, and his head was tilted back a little. Then he smiled very gently at the two of us.

'You should have gone,' he said. 'But it's all for the best now.'

He pointed to the main door which led to the staircase. 'Don't open the windows on to the verandah until I've opened that door,' he said, 'then creep out on to the verandah. I think it will give you time.'

From the courtyard below we could now hear the crack of rifle-shots. Then the thuds of battering against the outside Palace doors. The howls and shrieks outside seemed to stab into my ears.

'What are you going to do, Excellency?' Bordeini asked.

'When they've broken into the Palace?' the General answered. 'Go down to them.'

'They will not spare you,' Bordeini said.

'No,' the General replied quietly. 'But that is what must be. All things are ordained to happen. I will be killed. The Relief Expedition will have come too late. They will go back again.'

We could now hear the shrieks of the Palace servants as they fought to prevent the Dervishes from breaking in.

The General moved a little closer to the main door. Then he turned round to me.

'The words were true, Willie,' the General said. 'But two things I forgot. You have to pray to Him to give you strength—strength to resist many kinds of temptation. And you have to make sure that what orders your life is the true voice of God—and not your own self-righteousness.'

The General moved still closer to the door.

'Let me go with you,' I cried out.

The General gave me a long look. He stared at me as if he wanted to fix a picture of me in his mind. He smiled again, very gently.

'No, Willie,' he said. 'You must go back now to our forces.' Then he stopped as if he'd just remembered something. 'But I have one last order to give you,' he added.

The General walked quickly to the desk and picked up the ledger book which was lying on it. 'This is my journal,' he said. 'When you reach the Nile, tear out its pages and destroy them—every single one of them.'

Then he unlocked a drawer in the desk, and took out a wad of Egyptian bank notes. He crossed over to me. 'Here is the journal to destroy,' he said, handing it to me. 'Hide it beneath your shirt.' Then he handed me the bank notes. 'Here's all the personal money I've got left,' he said. 'Who can tell? It may help you along your way.'

He paused and stared at me once again.

In the silence I could hear Bordeini crying quietly.

'Are you ready for your journey, Willie?' the General asked.

'Yes, sir,' I said.

The noise from below grew louder. Suddenly there was a sound of splintering. The shrieks now seemed quite close.

'They're in,' the General said. 'Open the windows, Bordeini. You must move quickly.'

Bordeini unfastened the windows on to the verandah and opened them. From the direction of the river we could hear only faint cries and an occasional shot. The main force was obviously massed on the other side of the Palace, pressing into the hall below. As Bordeini turned from the windows the General could see his face.

'Don't cry,' the General said. 'I would we could all look on death as a friend who takes us from a world of bitter temptation to our true home.'

The General went up to the main door. Then he looked round at us.

'Go now,' the General said. 'God bless you both.'

Then he flung open the main door leading on to the head of the stairs. Immediately, there was a roar of noise from below. But when the General stepped out on to the landing, for an instant there was complete silence. It may have been the magnificence of his dress. It may have been the great fame of his reputation which, for that instant, silenced the Dervishes below. I don't know. But I believe it was the complete serenity of his expression.

'Come,' Bordeini whispered to me. 'Come now.'

But I couldn't move. I wanted to look at the General for the last time. He was standing there, gazing down into the hall with resignation. He stood in a calm and dignified manner, with his left hand resting lightly on the hilt of his sword.

'Quick,' Bordeini urged me.

But still I could not move. Even as I watched, suddenly the spell was broken. A tumult of screams and shouting burst out from the hall below. A few shots were fired.

I ran to the verandah. Then I turned back. I saw the General raise his right arm—just like I'd told Captain Brownlow, that Intelligence Officer at Korti. But it wasn't —as he'd suggested—'in a gesture of disdain'.

Even as the General saw the spear come plunging towards him, he stood with his right arm raised. But there was no disdain. He stood there in the attitude of someone who's been waiting a long time and has now lifted his arm to welcome a friend.